£ 4.99
100 ∨
19
2023)

**Allan Radcliffe** was born in Perth, Scotland, and now lives near Edinburgh. His writing has won the Allen Wright Award and the Scottish Book Trust New Writers Award. With an MA from the University of Glasgow, he works as an arts journalist and editor, and is currently a freelance theatre critic and feature writer. His short stories have been published in anthologies including *Out There*, *The Best Gay Short Stories* and *New Writing Scotland*, and broadcast on BBC Radio 4. *The Old Haunts* is his debut novel.

# The Old Haunts

ALLAN RADCLIFFE

Fairlight Books

First published by Fairlight Books 2023

Fairlight Books
Summertown Pavilion, 18–24 Middle Way, Oxford, OX2 7LG

A CIP catalogue record for this book is available from the
British Library

1 2 3 4 5 6 7 8 9 10

ISBN 978-1-914148-38-5

www.fairlightbooks.com

Printed and bound in Great Britain

Designed by Sara Wood

Illustrated by Sam Kalda

*For my family*
*and in memory of my mother,*
*Mary Radcliffe*

*The woods are lovely, dark and deep,*
*But I have promises to keep,*
*And miles to go before I sleep*

—'Stopping by Woods on a Snowy
Evening', Robert Frost (1923)

# We Don't Drink Beer

After the house was sold, we drove north to Aumrie, a cinematic place at the western end of Loch Tay. My head had been full of grey – a sky with no sunshine – and Alex thought the change of scene might help turn me back into myself.

It was March suddenly; the year was pulling at its reins. Alex had surprised me with a crumpled print-out, brandished like a long-stemmed rose. He knew our destination well, having grown up nearby, and he knew that I had taken that holiday there with my family. So, it was a meaningful place for both of us.

We kept pausing on the drive up so he could get out of the car with his camera and marvel at all his old haunts.

It was getting dark, the landscape receding, when Alex spotted the sign for the village and the White Waters. The apartment – one portion of a steading conversion – was waiting at the end of a mile-long track, the forest deepening on either side. Alex had to slow all the way down to avoid snagging the underside of the car.

He negotiated a sloping turn, his eyes turning to seeds as the Panda bumped down through a wrought-iron gate towards a paved yard. Pristine windows gleamed from old stone. Razor-edged slate shone from the sloped roof. Only the barns and outbuildings looked decrepit enough to be original feature.

Alex unfurled his legs from the car. A woman was making her way towards us: eager and waving with both hands.

'Mister and Missus Karim? Kit Ross. We met over the Internet!'

She was sixtyish, soft-faced with giant grips in her piled hair. She glanced over as I made my way around from the passenger side.

'This is Jamie, by the way,' Alex said, reaching behind him.

'It is so nice to meet you, Jamie.'

If she was taken aback by my not being a Missus, she didn't show it. I kept my hand welded to Alex's back as she led us to the furthest corner of the courtyard.

'You two look like you need to get inside and get your beers in the fridge.'

I heard flecks of something not of here in the way her voice went up at the end of each sentence.

'Oh, we don't drink... *beer*,' Alex said, flashing his fangs.

'You're the first of the season.' She moved into the vestibule, shouldering the interior door, snapping on the light. 'Folk don't usually start coming until Easter. You've pretty much got this whole neck of the woods to yourselves. There, now. I've got the place all cosy and warm for you.'

The apartment was compact, all on one floor with the kitchen and bathroom on one side of the hallway and the bedroom and living room on the other. Alex had to duck as we peeked through the bedroom door. I felt my limbs turn heavy at the sight of the king-sized bed, the bedspread pulled taut. Cotton-white walls, a lingering smell of paint: everything bland like a show house save for the mini-zoo of stuffed animals plonked along the window ledge. There were dogs, cats, a gorilla and a giraffe. Three bears, the baby nuzzled between its parents.

'It all looks very smart,' I said, following her into the kitchen. 'I don't know if I dare sit down, everything looks so new and clean.'

'What's that now?' Kit Ross was gazing up at Alex, her head tilted like a connoisseur. There are so few like him, with that hair, black like you've never seen black before, and his newsreader's voice. He had marched around the kitchen counter and was peering into cupboards, checking where

9

everything was. The clothes he wore accentuated his height: drainpipes, vertical stripes, and boots with pointed toes. One hand, the pink of his finger-nails peeking through chipped black, brushed mine as he came past.

We paused in the hallway while Alex dived into the bathroom to take a leak. Kit Ross took a breath and launched into an interrogation, her voice rising to cover the torrent. How was our journey? Had my friend and I visited before? Did we have plans? How was the weather in London?

We had spent the previous week in Edinburgh, I told her, though I stopped short of telling her why. For once, I hadn't noticed the weather.

'Look at those lashes!' She leaned forward, as though seeing me for the first time. 'Are those real?'

'They're my mother's,' I said, remembering my last-minute decision to put in my contacts. 'My dad said her eyelashes could have fanned Cleopatra.'

'Well, I can quite see that.'

Alex came back into the hallway and her attention once again floated upwards. 'It *was* the smaller apartment you booked?' she said. 'The *double* room?'

Alex lifted his chin. 'That's us.'

'That's fine,' I said, as though we were used to making do.

'Well, think of this as your home from home.'

She stole a final delighted look up at Alex. What did we look like to her, I wondered? Alex, with the stack of bracelets that hissed up and down his forearms. Me, peeping like Kilroy over the top of my rollneck. I thought of the estate agent who had visited the house before Christmas: a boy of twelve in an outsized suit. He held himself at arm's length throughout the appointment. One sudden flick of my limp wrist, I thought, and he would defend himself with his golf umbrella.

Alex frilled his fingers at Kit as she passed by the kitchen window at the back of the apartment. We heard a door unlocking and then the creak of her footsteps.

'My god, she really is right next door,' Alex said. 'We are going to have to make out *so quietly.*'

His roving eye alighted on the kitchen counter. 'Wow, is that shortbread?'

I unpacked and cooked while Alex got the fire going in the living room then walked his mobile around the apartment until it chirruped into life.

He cast an eye over the leaflets Kit had left.

'We could take a walk along the old railway line tomorrow. Have a go at finding this house of yours. I mean: if you think you're up to it?'

'I'm fine,' I said.

We took our bottle through to the fire and chose a DVD from the stack by the telly. The film was a romantic comedy about a woman who works selling train tickets. She's in love with one of her regulars but he doesn't notice her. Then, when he falls onto the platform and ends up in a coma and she's the first one on the scene, his family mistakes her for his girlfriend.

My mother would have called it an old cod. The ending would have given my father the excuse he needed to cry until all that came out was damp breath.

I pouted silently into my rollneck. Alex pulled my head onto his lap. 'I'm fine. I'm fine,' I said. He stroked my hair. It was almost a motherly embrace.


That night, as I was sitting up in bed and staring off, I felt him looking at me.

'I was thinking about my dad,' I said. 'I was trying to picture him. Just when I think I've got him clear in my head, it's like he shrinks and loses all his... dimensions, you know, like one of those wee men cut out of paper.'

Alex put aside his phone.

'I'm sorry I never got to meet them.'

'They were... good people.'

'I was twelve when my dad died,' he said. 'Someone – a teacher, maybe, or a neighbour or the priest, I can't remember now – said the only advantage of losing a parent at an early age is that you have less to forget. Or maybe that was something I read in one of the books. Anyway. Every time I see a picture of my dad, I notice something that surprises me. Like his freckles – the man had so many bastard freckles, across his nose. I must have seen them loads of times, but for some reason I don't think of my dad as a freckled person.'

He continued to watch me, wondering if his words had helped, as though a reminder of his loss could somehow draw me outside of my own.

I wanted to talk more, to tell Alex about my mum and my dad, he had such clear views on people and things. But which version to choose?

So, I changed the subject, complimenting him on his new haircut, which was shorter at the back and sides than usual, and he shrugged, kneading the thatch while glancing across at me a couple of times. I kissed him and told him goodnight before turning onto my side, and when I heard his breathing change I raised myself to my elbows. His sleeping face: it almost made me want to dig out my sketchpad just so I could draw him.

Outside the rain picked up. It rustled against the window.

The three bears watched from the window ledge.

*Somebody has been sleeping in my bed!*

I felt smaller than ever.

# One Day All This
# Will Be Yours

For a long time, we lived in the flat above my parents' newsagent's. The building was unique: a two-storey rectangular block, with no architectural kin close by. It was sandwiched between a tenement row and the forecourt of a Honda showroom. The outside had once approximated white but, one summer, when all the patches of grime had started joining up, my father cracked and painted the façade the only colour he had to hand. It changed shade more than once over the years, but it would be known forever after as The Purple Shop.

The front door opened onto the pavement. An aged swing sign blew back and forth on the street: *Come on in – it's all here.* Next to the main building was our garage; for years we had no car, so my dad stuffed the space with excess stock. Out the back there was a strip of green that could barely fit a whirligig, with a grid of slabs at the far end, which my mother optimistically referred to as The Patio.

The view from my bedroom window was of an advertising billboard, stuck to the side of the tenement block that ran perpendicular to our street. I opened my curtains onto faces with Aquafresh smiles or giant vodka bottles or dead-eyed cars.

Still, we were never far from history or damp greenery. If you turned right out of our front door and crossed the road, a cobbled close led through to Holyrood Park and the wall that ran along the back of the palace. If you walked to the top of the road that curved behind the car showroom you could see Arthur's Seat, the lounging giant, its head visible above the tenements and surveying the shoppers on London Road.

The Purple Shop creaked and groaned, needing repair. My mother killed her back oiling hinges and sticking down floorboards. 'One day, all this will be yours,' she muttered, while guddling around in the building's guts.

Lying in bed, I strained to listen to them moving around, chuckling at some mysterious joke, or sharing problems of a work–domestic nature that were beyond me. They seemed more than two people who shared a marriage and a shop. They were best friends, a double act, so close that the boundaries between them were almost irrelevant. I lay in the dark, open-eyed and indignant. When I couldn't sleep, they came through and sang 'Morningtown Ride', my father growling beneath her clear tones.

I was seven, and curious. I asked my mother how it was they had come to open the shop. It seemed such a bold thing to do, and so unlike them.

The usual pause while she considered the right way to tell the story.

'My dad, your granddad, moved out when I was your age, and your gran had to work more than one job. She said I never gave a thought to how hard her life had become.' She broke off, her face tightening. 'She was probably right.'

She had longed to get away, she told me. The afternoon she finished her Highers she caught the bus into the centre of town and walked up and down Princes Street and George Street, looking for signs in windows and asking at counters until she found a shoe shop that was looking for full-time staff.

'Your grandmother was... not happy,' my mother said. 'She had expected me to go to college, but I knew that would mean three or four or *five* years of listening to her telling me how untidy I made the place look, how much I cost her. When I told her I was planning to move out as soon as I had saved enough money to put down a deposit on a room, she went very quiet. I don't know why I was surprised. It was exactly what I had wanted to do: *wind her up.*'

She was talking almost to herself now.

'Anyway. She left me some money, her savings' – she made a noise somewhere between a cough and a sigh – 'and I, well, I think I wanted to prove something to myself or maybe even to honour her memory, who knows. So, I used it as the deposit for the shop. *There*.'

She straightened up, all business.

'You would have liked her. Your gran. She was a snappy dresser. She was always just so, no scuffs. Sharp tongue. Not like other people's grandmothers. She wasn't a sweetie. She didn't knit.'

I have a hazy half-recollection of the plaque with my father's name on it being drilled to the front of the shop. *Matthew James Haley*. As I get older, this memory, like so many things, begins to seem more like something I've been told.

I clung to the brightly lit shop. It meant warmth; it was home. The counter area was separated from the back room by a beaded curtain that brattled as the strings lifted and dropped into place. Dad would shout *'Jamie!'* as soon as he heard the click of the beads, and he would pull me into the armpit of the tweedy jacket he always wore, the one Mum kept holding up and saying had seen better days.

I breathed in his woody smell until he began to hold me away from him, loosening his grip: 'Ah'm gonnae drop ye.' Blue eyes cut in half by sleepy lids

– also my eyes, which were framed by my mother's famed lashes. I was theirs, no question.

At cashing up time, as the till churned out the day's receipts, I would sit through the back, scarfing crisps and doing homework or reading my way through the tied stacks of magazines. *Woman's Own*, *Woman's Weekly* and *The People's Friend*: I liked the fireside stories, the sleek photography and the cottagey illustrations. It was there, aged eight or nine, searching through a pile on the desk where my parents kept their paperwork, that I found a new title, *For Women*, and opened it. There was Todd, that month's full-frontal centrefold.

With his rigid hair and ludicrously square jaw, Todd looked like a cartoon hero – Fred from *Scooby-Doo* or a Disney prince – only with glossy pubes, a sponge-like scrotum and a belly that seemed to go on forever. The soft focus lent the image a dreamlike quality. Everything about Todd – his skin, his eyes – *shone*. I shut the magazine, breathed, then peeped again. Without thinking I tore him from the magazine, folded him at the waist and tucked him away; my heart thrilled. I knew this was something my parents wouldn't like; that it was something I should not be doing. Until then I had kept almost nothing from them. That leaf of flimsy paper was the first thing that came between us, the first in a career of secrets.

After dark I wore the page ragged, folding and unfolding until Todd ghosted away to nothing.

Before Todd, I read *The Beezer*, *The Broons*, books about children who solved crimes or went on journeys and ended up with their forever families. Mum read murder mysteries and the Sunday supplements. My father loved crossword puzzles, word searches and quizzes. When he was concentrating, he used to let his mouth hang open while he stroked his jawline. Friends were always telling him he should apply for *Mastermind* or *Fifteen to One*.

'Not for me,' he would say, 'I'm not one for being the centre of attention,' and, as if by way of demonstration, he would edge closer to my mother.

I don't know whether having me was always part of their plan. I have no idea if my arriving so late was just a happy accident or the result of years of trying. Last Chance Saloon was how I heard my mother describe me to her friend Maggie in a rare moment of confidence.

I didn't notice their age until I began comparing them to other people's parents. I didn't correct my classmates when they said 'your gran' this or 'your granddad' that.

But their grip was steel when they lifted me over the dogshit in the park.

As time passed, and his energies ebbed, my father gave up his spot at the end of the counter and took to sitting on a stool under the fags display with the puzzle pages spread out on the floor. He was so low down you could barely see the twirl of his hair from the door. Shoplifters ran riot. He still stroked his jawline, but it had become a kind of displacement activity, a means of keeping himself alert throughout shifts.

My dad knew many people and most of his friends had a smell you could taste. He was careful with money, having started out with nothing, a fact that continued to visit him in the night. But he had a generous streak. Whenever a pouch of tobacco burst, my dad gathered the coarse strands into the bags we used for penny sweeties. I lost track of the amount of free baccy he gave away, the number of times I heard him say, 'Ocht, don't be daft,' when Tony or Gordon or Maxie delved into their trouser pockets and made a big show of rattling their change. These men would go through the rigmarole of objecting, rounding their mouths, admonishing Dad for being too generous for his own good, too good for this world. His colour rose and his best wishes went with them to the door.

Once, when I was helping in the shop, because I had come of age and my parents were slowing,

I tried taking money from a man named Adie Morrison, who I knew fine well hadn't paid for his halves of Old Holborn since he lost his job as a gas fitter in the late eighties. It was a way of kicking against them, of showing my father that I was my own person. As I held out my hand Dad sprang like Zebedee from his berth behind the counter. Adie backed away, returning his damp fiver to his pocket, baccy and papers tight in his other fist.

My father glared at me.

'Won't. Do it. Again,' I recited, slamming the till, turning to grab up a 200-pack of Lambert & Butler, tearing into the paper. Dad blinked over at me, disorientated at having been forced to his feet so abruptly.

Now, every morning, after a shower, I conjure their ghosts. In the steamed mirror I see my father: we have the same outline, the same reddish-brown hair swirling above our faces; the same compact build. The close-up is my mother, with the pointed features and fair skin. So, he provided the frame, my mother the detail.

For a time, I played at being him. I'd stand in front of the bathroom mirror and square my shoulders. I knew I could pass if I tried hard enough.

I also tried out the quiet tones of my mother's make-up, though I could never capture her subtle look. I always went too far, forgetting myself, scrubbing at the pancaked layer whenever my father tapped at the bathroom door, asking to be let in.

It wasn't until a few years later, long after I had moved away, that I realised I could make my childhood into stories for other people's amusement. I have always drawn, and I especially love drawing people. My portraits are sometimes cartoonish, whether out of affection or spite, or they can be hyper-realistic, but I have always tried – I have *tried* – not to make my parents into caricatures.

They sold The Purple Shop in the mid-noughties and moved to a slender new build. There was another newsagent's by then, further up the street, and a warehouse of a Sainsbury's in the nearby retail park. So eventually our old building was converted into two flats. Mum and Dad, who went on the same walk every day, circling the park with an impatient tread, regularly found themselves on our old street. At some point both flats went on the market again but stayed unsold. Their report was always the same: the front door was padlocked, and the windows painted over.

The day after my mother's funeral I took Alex to visit the now-legendary shop only to discover that it was gone. No rubble. Just a larger than usual gap between the tenements and the car lot, but nothing you would notice if you weren't looking for it. Almost as though it had never existed. I had to walk up and down the street to make sure I hadn't made a mistake.

We stood around on the pavement squinting into the surprisingly small gap while I tried my very damnedest to redraw the imprint of the shop in my head. It was a mild day for December, and we were eating ice cream, treacherously bought from the supermarket. I took a step back to the kerb so I could see properly. There was the Honda show-room, its chain-and-bollard fence red with rust, but still holding strong. The neighbouring tenements stood huddled together like fearful old men. There was the billboard, today warning of a brand-new American sitcom. Already some comedian had spray-painted a cock and balls across one of the actors' foreheads.

I felt as though the world had changed, but subtly, as though it had been tilted or shifted a few degrees.

# A Book of Fairy Tales

Something woke me: a beat or a breath. For a couple of scary moments, I tried to locate familiar things.

We had come on holiday, that was it. We'd fetched up in a room filled with teddies in someone else's house in the middle of a forest.

Alex was here. He was right next to me.

Alex, bumphled in the covers, was trying to speak in that dream way: like his mouth was sewn shut. '*Mhhhh.*'

'Alex.'

He put a hand on his chest, his gasps turning to breathed laughter. '*Ahh,*' he said. '*Ah-haha!*' His heart, like a drill. He turned over, and I felt him spread and settle once again. Enjoy this, I told myself. Enjoy him. But I was alert now, fixated on the mass of dark between the bed and the door. There was nothing to see but I lay there for who knows how long, trying to make the darkness move like water.

*

I soon found myself at the kitchen table, turning pages, the room quiet around me. The book was *A Treasury of Fairy Tales*. My parents' message, etched in biro, was still just visible across the top of the first page: *To Jamie, Happy 5$^{th}$ Birthday, Love from Mummy and Daddy xx.*

When I found this book in a drawer in their house, the worse for wear but intact, I had hugged it like it was a living thing. The dust jacket was gone. I could barely remember the cover illustration. The book had forever been known as the Blue Book for the colour of its binding. I had always loved its frightening pictures. To this day it conjures bedtime safety, the delight of fear.

For now, it was consolation. When I opened the book, my parents came wafting into the room. They were such careful people, but they could never think of cigarettes as dangerous. Sometimes I would hide their fags, relenting only after they had torn the place apart in agitation.

*Don't lecture, Jamie. You are a child.*

*But I don't want you to die.*

*We are not going to die.*

I remember sitting cross-legged in bed, listening to them on the other side of the wall. They were worrying about something. They worried about everything. A picture came into my head: Hansel and Gretel with their arms around each other, their doll-features filled with terror, listening at the top of the stairs as the woodcutter and his wife hatched their plot to abandon the children in the woods.

How old would I have been? Nine or ten? I had long carried around this night-time loneliness, a hatred of separation; a vague sense that life could change for the worse quickly and without warning.

Now I heaved up the book and scoured until I found the right page. I gazed like a fond father at the children's hamster cheeks.

*'What are we going to do now?' said the little boy. 'We're all alone.'*

I had been sitting in my T-shirt and pyjama trousers and I was cold. My eyes were drawn to a hanging photograph of what turned out to be an aerial shot of the steading in the middle of the forest, in snow. The clearing looked so secluded that suddenly my loneliness magnified. I looked away from the picture, sleepy now, too long away from Alex, and at that moment I heard something, some subdued movement from upstairs. Feet padding right above my head then descending in a careful rhythm, settling somewhere to my right.

The creaking stopped and I heard someone start speaking. At first I thought the radio had come on but then I realised it was her, the woman, what was her name again, Kit, the steady up-and-up of her voice; a muffled monologue in which all the words seemed to run together without pause. I imagined her padding around, still with her hair bundled on top of her head. A gap and then I heard her blurt laughter at something or someone I couldn't see.

Outside, the forest sighed.

# Make Light

I cannot remember many conversations that didn't come back round to money. I have a memory of my parents sitting hunched over their books long into the evening, lost in fine margins, raddled by constant effort.

It was obvious when things were bad because they would turn me out of the kitchen where the accounts were piled on the table. Before the door closed on me, I caught glimpses of their worry. It was in the way my mother scratched at her arms; the way that my dad's face instantly grew thinner. Over time I saw the extent of it. They didn't have to tell me that all this work and worry was for my sake.

They brought out the best tumblers for guests but otherwise treats were handed out sparingly. 'You want half an apple with me?' my father would say. 'Mouthful of juice?' 'Square of chocolate?' Clothes were mended, never replaced. I watched how they skimped, and this made me hoard the coins in my plastic till like a miser.

When I moved away, my friends marvelled at how I could make a beer last the night. To this day I keep contingencies in drawers and tins and zip pockets.

Everything in moderation. When my parents said that they liked a drink, they meant it literally: one glass of a Saturday evening, maybe three at Christmas. Their drinks cabinet – a compartment of the sideboard – was full of bottles with mouldering labels. Once, seeing a half-empty bottle of sherry on the kitchen counter, I had an impulse to grab it up and take a gulp. For some reason I had expected the taste to be sweet: my father had been using it to make his trifle. The drink's heat made me gasp. The aftertaste was a reprimand. I ran to the sink, let the tap run and soused my tongue.

I asked my father about his parents. What were they like?

'Oh, I wish they'd lived to meet you, they'd have loved you.'

His face slowly tightened.

'I mean, I wouldnae ever say they were the most *reliable* of folk. We had to move around a wee bit. We had to flit in the night sometimes. I mind carrying a bag of stuff up the road to my uncle's because my old boy was behind on the rent, and we were out the door. Boxing Day. My hands were like ice.'

He mimed lifting the world's tiniest violin to his chin and played.

I asked him why his father kept losing his job.

'Drink. I mean, they all took a drink: his old boy, his brothers and all his friends, that's just what they liked to do.'

He held his head to one side.

'The thing is, Jamie, your grandfather was deep down a very shy man who wanted people to like him. It's that simple. It's that… daft. The drink made that easier. It made him less… fearful.'

I stared, none the wiser.

'He wasnae a bad man,' my father said. 'It seemed to me that my old boy took a drink the way other folk brushed their teeth or mucked out their lugs. He just wouldnae have felt his self without it.'

Their local – called the Scaffold but affectionately known as the Scaffy – sat on a corner at the top of the hill. It was famous for its folk club, which met in a room at the back of the pub. Until I was old enough to fend for myself, my parents took it in turns to get dressed up and climb the hill on a Thursday evening. They came home humming 'Mary Hamilton' and 'She Moved Through the Fair', an aura of smoke around them. I wasn't allowed to go up the road and peer through the door, so the folk club became an illicit thing: something to be wondered at and resented.

Fridays at the end of the month, when the group was counting its pennies, meant carry-out nights. Sometimes these took place in our flat, feet trampling the stairs and cans rattling in the hallway. Adie Morrison brought his guitar and people would sing traditional songs and sixties standards that grew louder and more porous as the night wore on. If he were well-enough jaked, Adie would launch into his party piece: all seventeen thousand verses of 'Sad-Eyed Lady of the Lowlands'. The voice that came out of him was too big for his thin frame.

I didn't like the Sad-Eyed Lady. She outstayed her welcome and no one knew when to start the applause. Carry-out night felt like an invasion. I was expected to sit quietly in my own home, and I was never allowed to put on my one and only album, a selection of 1991's biggest chart hits. On Saturday mornings when my parents were downstairs opening up, I wore that record out. When the shop was all finished with for the day, my father joined in lip-synching along to 'The One and Only'. He pushed his shoulders back and sang into an invisible mike or made windmills with his hands. My mother lit up with laughter. My dad squinted at the album sleeve. 'These are the year's number ones? More like number twos, most of them.'

I swiped at his arm. I wanted nothing more than this.

My mother had this incredible full-throated chuckle. And when my father laughed his whole head went back. Seeing them like this, limp with laughter, made me want to keep telling them the best joke they'd ever heard. I had seen that they were often wound tight with worry. Now I thought it was my job to make light, to lighten them.

'Let there be light!'

My dad said it every evening when he turned on the big lamp in the living room, splaying his fingers like a magician.

On carry-out nights my parents sat at the end of a row of pals who also sang, in groups or alone. They nursed drinks in proper glasses, occasionally joining in on a verse and a chorus, clinging onto the underside of the sofa when Adie Morrison did his party piece. Good whisky appeared and the bottle floated around the room. I was on the floor at my mother's feet in nice clothes. I spent a lot of time fiddling with her shoes: lacing and unlacing, until the press of her hand on my shoulder told me to stop.

They weren't religious people, but this was their church. Some of the congregation called me the Wee Man and gave me surprisingly tender pats on the shoulder as they came in the door. Where are they now? Gordon. Maxie. Isobel. I recall incidents, the odd recurring phrase.

Talk often turned to politics. All my parents' friends were Labour, even the ones who didn't work. To me, Labour meant Christmas parties in Tranent; pushing red leaflets through letterboxes in Lochend and Portobello, hoping dogs wouldn't take the ends off my fingers. For my parents Labour meant always being prepared for life's many disappointments. They flew the red flag more out of habit than principle. 'Ocht well,' they said, when they woke to see John Major waving and grinning from the steps of Number Ten. And then the dial on the telly would be turned and the dread thing would disappear, replaced in its slot by something safer, easier to thole.

Councillor Waddell made regular appearances at carry-out nights. He flitted from group to group, the knot of his tie protruding over the neck of his red jumper. He held a bottle of lager, which he waved in the air as he talked. With his pink hands and expressive eyes, he included every member of the group in what he was saying.

I had heard my mother's friend Isobel whispering that she thought Councillor Waddell was a little light in his loafers. I stared at his brogues, unclear what she meant.

One night, enjoying the intensity of his listening face, I realised with a thump that he had turned slightly and was looking at me. There was a split second of uncertainty, during which I sat rigid. Then his lips separated into a grin of recognition. He bounded over.

'Can it be Jamie? Your mother must have put you in the grow bag.'

I could feel her gently prodding my back.

'Yes. I mean... thanks,' I said.

'Tell Councillor Waddell your news,' my mother chimed.

He bent his head. I was ten years old; there wasn't much to report. I felt my parents behind me, rigid with pride. My mother's whispered prompts slipped over my shoulder: *Science project. Short story competition. History test.*

Councillor Waddell straightened up, gathering in my parents with his eyes.

'Bravo. Good for you, Jamie,' he said. 'Louie and Matthew, you must be very proud of this boy.' He held out his bottle of lager to tap against my lemonade and, as the glass chinked, I accidentally let go a cackle of pleasure.

Councillor Waddell made the front page of the *Evening News* some years later. The article said he had been discovered performing a sex act on another man in the woods next to a play park. I was in my final year at school; the incident coincided with the row over the repeal of Section 28 so for a while the two stories were laid side by side in people's minds like some basic equation, further confirmation if any were needed that homosexuality was wrong, deceitful, a threat to young people.

My parents were reluctant to talk about what had happened. I wanted to know more about what Councillor Waddell had been doing in those woods. I asked my mother if he and his wife were still together.

She took her time in answering.

'Helen Waddell. She's a mousey wee thing. I can't imagine how she must be feeling.' She shook her head. 'Rotten bugger.'

My mother rarely if ever swore.

# Keanu's Eyes

'Alex?' I wrestled free from the duvet and blankets, a childish feeling in my belly.

But he was there, perched in the kitchen, the damp thatch combed back from his face.

'Did you sleep okay?'

'I'll have a guid rest in my grave.'

It was my father's phrase. I reeled it off without thinking but for some reason it never failed to make Alex honk with laughter.

'How long did you say we've got this place for?' I asked him.

'I've booked it for the week. When are you due back?'

'Bannerman told me I could take as long as I needed.'

I had gone back to work ten days after my mother's funeral. I told myself I was fine. For a while, I *was* fine; I looked very much like business as usual.

It was lunchtime and the canteen was mobbed, voices haggling, heads bobbing. A colleague saw me standing in the middle of the floor, leaning at an impossible angle. I had forgotten some detail: the exact way my mum held her hand to her chest when she laughed or my father's habit of soothing his nose with his finger when he took off his glasses. I wanted so much to remember.

The kids had noticed. Apparently, there had been sniggers, some gawping. Bannerman appeared and huckled me into her office.

'Do you have someone, a, well, a, a friend, you'd like me to call and have come and pick you up?'

I hadn't been that physically close to Bannerman since my interview six years earlier. Afterwards, she had come out of her office to tell me the job was mine and I had immediately found a quiet corner to phone my parents.

Did she remember now what had happened? Was she listening when I told her my mum and dad were gone? Did their goneness matter? Or was I just a name on a rota, a pair of words, 'James' and 'Haley', to be shifted around, replaced at short notice, deleted?

'Are you feeling okay, Jamie?' she said.

*I feel like I've got something heavy in my head. A brick maybe. Make that a boulder. A great fuck-off boulder. Rocks in my chest and stones in my throat. And they keep getting bigger and heavier.*

*And the heaviness makes me feel tired. And I wish*
*they would either shrink away or just blow up too*
*big for my insides. I wish they would just burst,*
*breaking me open, letting my insides spill out onto*
*your nice beige carpet. All that anger, all sadness*
*gone. That would feel good, I think. I'd like that,*
*sure. I'd feel... I'd feel light again.*

'I'm fine,' I said. 'I'll be fine.'


I left her office just as the bell rang. Bannerman
had suggested, in her classroom voice, that I take
time off, and I had said yes, why not, yes, with a
little inward slump. Doors slammed open on either
side of the corridor, rooms disgorging teenagers. I
started heading slowly towards the main exit. This
had been six years of my life.

When I was halfway across the schoolyard the
sun came out with a sudden fierce heat. I haven't
felt this light in ages, I thought as I speed-walked
through the gates.


'We need to get you back into a routine,' I heard
Alex say.

Like a child. Like an old person.

I crossed my arms, pretending not to have heard.


A couple of nights before we came north, we had
lolled on our bed in the Alba Guest House in
Edinburgh, sorting through books of photographs.

'I haven't seen some of these before,' I said, still wired to the gills on the adrenaline of that long week, flushed with the achievement of emptying the house.

There was my father, his bulk in soft focus, leaning against a cannon at Stirling Castle, one elbow resting on her barrel. A smile so shy it made my heart float. Their wedding photo: they looked like kids in outsized clothes. The three of us, me in the middle: rotund, fastened to my mother. From the age of five onwards, my TV-screen glasses became such a permanent feature that I lost sight of what my face looked like without them.

A school photo, the year carved into the top of the cardboard frame: 1999. There I was, fifteen and made of secrets, cross-legged on the floor, the smallest boy in my class, my blanked eyes not quite obscured by curtains of hair.

Alex held it to his face, glancing between the two versions.

There was still a sense that what had happened wasn't real, that it was reversible even, that the pictures were as good as the real thing. My mother had labelled her photographs: *Louie's Parents*, *Matthew's Parents*, *Jamie Baby Photos*, *Jamie School Photos*, *Holidays*, *Our Friends*. For a long time afterwards, I kept these albums handy. Sometimes I would take them down and look at them. To remind me: *Ah, that's what they looked like. Weren't they gorgeous?* But only for a moment: the way a daft laddie might hold a lit match to his skin just long enough to register pain.

'You go and get your armour on,' Alex said. 'I'll get our boots from the car.'

His bracelets shinked up his arm as he ruffled his hair into shape. I saw him smile to himself, anticipating the day's pleasures, and I had this sudden urge to pull him onto my lap, drag him to bed, beg him to let us spend the day in our jammies.

How long had we been together now – ten, eleven months? Perilously close to a year. He used to come into Ground Up in Bayswater where a few of us from school would gather for lunch on a Friday. He and the rest of the team from the cleaning company would be there at the same table by the window at the end of their shift, giggling wearily into their lattes.

I noticed his height and the rose-gold of his skin, the piercings, and that military way he carried himself with his shoulders back and his chin out.

One day, as I ate, I caught him looking past his friends, finding my eyes. Suddenly he was a different person, minus the comic-book sheen.

I joined him at the counter when he went up to pay.

'Quieter the day,' he said, and there it was, the accent.

'You're Scottish?'

He told me later that he liked my shyness, my geeky specs, the way I rabbited when I was nervous. I couldn't flirt for toffee, so I ended up firing questions at him, creasing with laughter at pretty much everything he said.

He told me he was an actor. 'Can't you tell?' he said, flapping the front tail of his tabard.

As I was gathering my things to leave the café, I could see him watching me in the mirror that hung over the counter. One of those faces you just want to look at: cheekbones, Keanu's eyes. When I finished for the day, he was hovering outside the school, leaning against his bike handlebars. He had followed me.

'Look, do you want to...?' He thumbed over his shoulder.

'Yeah,' I said, stumbling like a toddler, literally throwing myself at him.

We went back to his flat in Stoke Newington. There was music as soon as we walked through the door. Big voices, singing *Willkommen!* Something from a musical, maybe. I couldn't work out if he'd switched on the stereo with the light or whether it had been on all the time he was out.

I told him I liked musicals, oh yes, loved them, and he raised his eyebrows at me. I searched my head, but the only name that came to me was *Starlight Express*.

'Get out of my house,' he said.


His torso seemed designed to slot into his lower half like the plastic trunk of an action figure. He slapped a palm down on his stomach and joked that it would take him nine months to grow a beard.

He saw that I was self-conscious about my middle, this podge I sometimes get, and he let his lips linger. Before climbing on top, he asked did I mind if he came on my belly. He might have been asking if he could open the window and let in some air.

*Look at me*, he said. *Look at me*. We came one after the other, a pair of controlled explosions. We clung to each other like a couple of happy drunks.


I made my thrice-weekly phone call to my parents a couple of nights later. I had to cut the conversation short because I was running late to meet him.

The line went quiet.

'Don't think we know an Alex, do we? Where's he come from?'

*I come from the kingdom on the other side of the forest.*

'I'm sure I must have mentioned him before.'

My tone was devil-may-care, and of course they couldn't see my great big grin.

# What Have You Done with Jamie?

I can't know now what they would have made of him. I would have loved for them to meet him, and to like him. It took them a while to adjust to new things. As they grew older, the world increasingly frightened them, and they were often afraid for me.

Lately, I have found myself thinking about Maggie and Rory Falconer, who were old friends of my parents. They were adventurers, uninhibited, everything my parents were not. According to my mother the Falconers had caught the wanderlust while travelling around Europe on a scooter. Every few years they moved somewhere else, which meant gifts for me from Spain, Italy and Greece. For a long time, my plaster replica of the Parthenon was my most precious thing. I didn't dare take it into school in case someone snatched it or knocked it onto the floor.

Maggie was slight – Mum called her neat – with a sharp face and hair that fell heavily down her back. She complained of the cold and sat with her knees drawn up to her chest, huddling her shoulders.

It wasn't Maggie's angular features that fascinated me, or the way her eyes narrowed when she was listening. It was her voice. She spoke with an actor's authority. When I asked Mum if her friend had ever been on the telly, she laughed.

'Maggie McAllister went to the same school as your dad and me,' she said, as though this was an immediate barrier to any kind of career in the performing arts.

If I aspired to be Maggie, I wanted something else from Rory, though I couldn't have put those feelings into words. He was tall and dark with ears that stuck out at the sides of his head. Unlike Maggie, Rory was posh, having been to what my dad called one of the *privet* schools. His voice was a mix of rounded vowels and glottal stops, as though he'd spent his adult life trying to hide something in it: his privileged upbringing, maybe, or an adolescent tremor. He dressed for comfort, rotating a handful of round-collared shirts, and his hair alternated between huge and unkempt or cropped so close it might have been drawn onto his head in charcoal.

I was afraid of how he made me feel.

Rory had a big, open face that got sectioned off into compartments whenever he smiled. There was a ritual I loved where, upon arrival, he would pick me up and throw me over his shoulder and carry me about the flat like a Santa sack, shouting: *Where's Jamie? What have you done with Jamie?*

I clung on, shrieking: the world upside-down.

My parents were different around these Falconers. They seemed younger, lighter. Mum loved to sit and listen to Maggie's stories about the crazy driving in Italy or the chaos and beauty of Barcelona. She would beg for a half-hour's respite if I were hovering nearby. 'Why don't you find something to do?'

'This boy has no interest in making friends,' I heard her say, and through the doorway I saw her droop. And I thought: I will make friends, or I'll pretend to her that I have friends, and then she won't have to worry about me.

She and Maggie went back to talking about their youth. The best of times. The sixties had stuck to Maggie. She used phrases like 'dream on' and 'no great shakes' without irony. Later, my mother would admit to me that the version of the sixties that made it to her part of the world was anaemic compared to the stark etching on the cover of the *What We Did on Our Holidays* album.

My father and Rory showed their affection for one another in the only way they knew how: shadow boxing or cuffing each other on the back of the head. They drank beer with their knees almost but not quite touching, eyes wet with laughter. Rory would reach a point in the evening when the beer would make him sentimental, and they would find round-about ways to express their mutual appreciation.

Rory admired the way my father had walked out of a dull job as a warehouseman to take on his own business.

'Selling Regal and cola bottles isnae what you'd call rewarding,' my father said. 'Teaching's a useful job. You're nurturing eager minds.'

'I teach Athenians elementary-level English,' Rory said. 'Talking with your hands and Cuisenaire rods. It's not exactly *Goodbye Mr Chips*.'

I always knew when the Falconers were due because my father would take all his camping and hiking equipment down from the loft and make an inven-tory on the living room floor: two-man tent, poles and pegs, mallet, duct tape, sleeping bags.

When they pitched up in their little Italian car, I knew I had to make the most of my time with Rory because he and my dad would soon be setting off up north.

Mum and Maggie watched them leave from my bedroom window.

'Look at that pair,' said Maggie as Rory executed a rapid three-point turn, one hand on the wheel, pointing the car's nose towards London Road, the New Town and the Forth Bridge. 'Like a couple of wee boys.'

I would have been about ten – still young but no longer small enough to be lifted onto Rory's shoulders – when the Falconers' marriage ended. We hadn't seen them together for a while, though Rory had visited alone in the summer to go camping with my dad and Maggie had dropped in on her way to visit her mother. When Mum dropped into the conversation that they were to separate I cried inconsolably.

'It's just one of those things,' said my mother.

What was she on about? This was change, real and terrible.

It was only later, thinking about their visits, that I realised I had always known on some level that Maggie and Rory weren't together in the way my parents were. It was something to do with the way they could be in the same room, always looking just past each other. They came as a pair, and yet as soon as they were through the door they seemed to separate, Maggie making a beeline for my mother while Rory and Dad went through their burly embrace. When one of them was speaking, the other stared at the floor, drawn to some fascinating detail in the carpet.

We only saw Maggie a couple more times after they split. She told us she was sick of teaching and wanted to move closer to her mother. Closer meant Brighton, about as far from the central belt of Scotland as you could get and still be on the same island. The first time I saw her post-Rory she looked different. Her hair was shorter, cut along the jawline. She seemed self-conscious in it, as though she'd got dressed in the dark and made a grab for the wrong wig.

'I like your hair.' It was all I could think of to say. She lifted a hand to the side of her head, a flicker of loss crossing her face.

'Not too drastic, is it?'

'It's neat,' I said.

When in doubt I channelled my mother.

The summer before I started high school, we all three drove out to meet Rory at the airport. He was stopping over for a couple of hours on his way to Rio de Janeiro. Mum made me find Brazil on the plastic globe that lit up when it was plugged in. I had never been to the airport before. My father set off early so we could sit in the car in a layby somewhere watching the planes taking off and coming in to land.

Dad was quiet when we got to the terminal and met Rory in the coffee shop. I thought his handsomeness was starting to blur. When his plane was called my father went to shake his friend's hand while Rory curled his arm around my father. They laughed and sprang apart; afraid someone might have witnessed such a display.

A letter came from Rory. My mother ripped the envelope and a bundle of photographs scattered across the table. Rory had met an American woman in Brazil and was now living with her on Staten Island, New York. His girlfriend had a thirteen-year-old boy who played all the sports and could give Rory a run for his money with what he called a soccer ball.

In the photos they were bunched together, all three, like they were made for each other.

'Rory a parent, can you imagine?'

My father stared. 'Looks like he's put on the beef.'

We hadn't seen him make an inventory of his camping equipment for a while. The highest peak he climbed now was Arthur's Seat, which he did a couple of times a week, lumbering out across the park, leaning into the hillside.

The box with the tent and poles and pegs didn't come down from the loft until we moved out of the flat. The Falconers faded away. Together they had been like a mirror version of my mother and father:

the freewheeling, do-what-you-feel variety. Apart, their connection to my parents made little sense. Now they disappeared so completely I might as well have made them up.

I think I was twelve years old on that morning of change when we gathered around the ripped-open parcel from Rory. A quick calculation tells me that my parents would have been in their mid-fifties. But in my memory, I'm still knee-high to them and they are giants. Time makes everything out of scale.

# The Warmest Welcome
# in Central Scotland

Alex was leaning over the car, studying the map. In the night the rainfall had made impressive puddles. Birds flickered past the wall of the steading like static on a screen. I tottered out onto the courtyard in my new boots: a kid trying out his mother's heels for the first time.

At the top of the slope we had a choice: turn right and go back down towards the village or left and up the hill where the track slunk away through the trees.

Alex propped himself against the leaning gateway, squinting at the map, turning it on its side. He looked pristine in his yellow raincoat and black beanie: a catalogue idea of a rambler.

'Okay. This is the way to the old railway line. Up here.'

The track narrowed as we clambered upwards. Trees leaned in every direction, straining to listen. The path quickly became so clogged we had to keep to the centre, avoiding the murky ovals. Where the dark water overwhelmed the waymarked trail, we clung to the overgrown edges.

*It's just mud – you can't get away from mud.* I was always prissy about getting my hands dirty. My mother sighed whenever I fell in the park and the tears started. She scooped me up. 'You're a sook,' she said. 'You're a softy.'

I have a memory of her sliding on a mat of mud and falling the length of herself as she walked me home from school. She tore a hole in the knee of her trousers and had to hobble all the way back with me trailing along behind her. I tried to take her hand, love inflating my insides.

'Try not to make a fuss, Jamie.'

She walked on, whistling to show me that it was nothing.

I heard Alex whistle a warning. He'd taken his camera out of its case and was aiming the lens just as I was attempting a Tarzan manoeuvre over a swamped stretch by way of a low-hanging branch.

I squirmed around, one leg sliding out behind me, attempting to rearrange my features into something worthy of his Facebook. I let go the branch and it pinged upwards, releasing a barrage.

'Fuck.'

*Click.*

This part of the forest was solid-walled, airless, the colour a generalised grey. I blindly followed Alex. A fingerpost saying *LOCH* appeared from behind a tree, causing me to curse so loud that Alex wheeled round.

'You okay there?'

'Scared of my own shadow.'

'There must be a way through here,' said Alex, pulling out the map. 'Yeah, no, okay, sorry, that's right. The path we want meets us at the other end of the forest.'

He remembered me again, turning, his boots slurping out of the mud. He extended a hand. I heard the drizzle crackling in the jaggies beside me.

'Come on. It'll be grand, let's get our legs going. Let's get over to the loch before it starts to pish down.'

*It'll be grand.* He said the same thing when he asked me to live with him. We were sitting in a corner of the bar at the National Film Theatre and Alex was leaning over the table with the intensity of a card shark. We had just been to see a Mike Leigh film. He was in it, playing a barman. We had to wait until the cinema was almost empty before we saw his name come up in the credits.

I didn't answer right away. We hadn't been together very long. It was just after my dad died.

Living together was a change I wasn't sure I was ready for.

'Come on, it'll be an adventure.'

For a while I had thought him confident, bordering on cocky. It had taken a while to notice the crinkles of uncertainty around his eyes.

*It'll be grand.* I contemplated his fringe, the hair so black it looked blue under the light, the way his jaw jutted out from the lower part of his face, the two sides coming together in a deep cleft. He seemed genuinely unaware of his insane beauty.


'So, I'm ninety-nine per cent sure your house is just up ahead.'

We had finally come out of the trees onto a vague trail that ran alongside what he said must once have been the old railway line. He strode ahead, quickening his pace as the path widened, embankments rising on either side.

'Yep, just through here,' he said, and he jinked to his left.

Gone.

I jogged to keep up, turning where I had seen him turn. I found myself clodhopping against concrete, the slabs already scattered with the mulch from his boots. A sign rose out of the ground: *Fairmount.* I shrank back as a car revved past, its engine labouring as it negotiated the ascent.

Fairmount was apparently a small estate with boxy new builds stacked all the way up the hill and ending in a cul-de-sac that looped around like a noose. Alex craned his neck, his eyes following the curve of the street to where it plunged back down towards the loch.

'What did you say the house looked like?'

'It was a… just a white cottage.' I made the vague shape of a rectangle with my hands. 'On its own on the hillside, with a clear view over to the loch and the hills. Solid, you know, but very… quaint. You could see it from all over.'

He stretched and tried to see over the tops of houses, to whatever might be hiding behind the shoulder of the hill.

'You went there just the once…' he said.

'I remember it so well,' I said, abruptly, as though trying to convince myself that the house did in fact exist. 'I had a big room to myself, it felt huge, and I remember seeing all kinds of things in the dark.'

'Nightmares?'

'My mother said I had an overactive imagination. Beasties behind the curtains and things with fangs at the end of the bed. I never wanted to be left alone.'

Alex looked at me.

'I had to share a room with one of my brothers, Mikey,' he said, 'and then one day he stomped off to live with a friend – he was seventeen and he loathed

57

my parents. I was the last one to fly the coop. It was the only time I had them to myself.'

His face twinged. Again, I found myself thinking how little I knew of him, that we had barely scratched the surface.

He took my hand, lifting his eyes to meet mine.

'Maybe you misremembered?'

'How do you mean?'

'The house. We're talking, what, twenty years ago?'

'Maybe,' I said, tilting my head. 'I really wanted to show you.'

We ran down to the loch, arriving at a car park and picnic stop that looked to have been hacked out of the hillside. Alex bee-lined to the toilets and dived inside while I loitered by a bench. There was a park with goalposts at the top of the grassy rise, a couple of swings and a climbing frame, daffs and crocuses everywhere.

The sun had come out, dispersing the clouds, sharpening the irregular line of the hillside beyond. Alex took the inevitable selfie with the loch and the hills in the background. 'We'll send it to my mum.' He smiled at his phone. 'Guess. Where. We. Are.'

I glanced around before putting an arm around him. Like there was anyone down here who would see or give the slightest fuck.

In Aumrie we stopped and watched the falls, the veiny lengths of white zigzagging all the way to the rubble-stone bridge that we had seen in all those films and ads for Visit Scotland. Alex detached himself and clambered down on to the rocks, one arm out for balance, the other pinning his camera to his side as the water made ineffectual grabs for his feet.

'Alex...'

More than once I had to stop and regain myself on ledges of rock or feel my way along the verge. Alex bounded out of reach, the shimmering spray between us.

The other side of the bridge was tourist-pretty, the effect only disrupted by the fact of a Co-op on the ground floor of one of the solid old houses, the usual overflowing recycling bank in the gap site next door.

A sign outside the Queen's Hotel told us to expect *The Warmest Welcome in Central Scotland*.

'Since 1879, no less,' Alex said.

'Since Christ came to Kirkcaldy.' He turned, his face a question. 'Oh, my dad, my dad,' I said.

The framed menu on the wall was trimmed with tartan. I caught my breath at the prices, then remembered the pile of money sitting in my account, the scant comfort of the two hundred grand I hadn't earned.

It was dead inside, just one table occupied by a family with a squad of kids, the parents slumped and defeated-looking. A teenager stared at Alex gliding through, turning to share a smirk with a younger girl. As he reached their table Alex clocked the toddler in her highchair and made a big face, to the child's enchantment. The mother tetchily admonished the older kids.

When I was out with Alex there was always attention. Strangers rubbernecked, catching my glare before finally moving past.

One day we passed a group of young white boys, barely high school age, on the street. '*Paki*,' one of them said, quietly but with feeling. The word came at me like a fist. But Alex strode on, and I couldn't then bring myself to ask whether he had heard.

We settled on the furthest corner where the floorboards gave way to yet more tartan. Rough-hewn beams slanted across the ceiling. There was green leatherette upholstery. The only thing out of place was the music.

'Streisand,' Alex said. 'How did they know we were coming?'

'My dad was a big fan. He loved all the divas: Dusty, Aretha, Diana... We used to gang up on my mum when we went on holiday. We made her listen to our tapes in the car. We sang our heads off. Oh, and her face...'

The memory spun through me: a vivid reel. I laughed, lightly at first and then almost violently, all the pent-upness shuddering up and out.

'Jamie...'

His eyes made an appeal. I batted back a goofy grin.

As we opened our menus, I noticed someone half-hidden on the other side of the bar. A face lifted, and then whoever was there was smiling, sliding down from a stool, waving with both hands.

'Oh, you're here!'

Kit Ross sank down next to Alex, who flinched at her proximity. She held out her half pint at arm's length.

'Just the ticket.'

Her eyes flicked between us: eyes the colour water goes when you add just a dropper of blue ink.

I began explaining our search for the house.

'I had this very clear memory of it being up on that hill overlooking the loch,' I said, 'but now I'm starting to doubt myself.'

'I used to be so proud of my memory,' Kit Ross said. 'Lately I've become shocked at how wrong I get the detail of things.'

Alex leaned across and reeled off my description of the house while Kit made suggestions. At times she seemed to be just looking at him, not really listening, just gazing, and thinking her own thoughts. Her laughter lines were so deeply etched they stayed in place even when her face was at rest.

'So many of those holiday homes stand empty during the winter,' she said. 'Such a waste. The clever folks saw this whole Airbnb thing coming and got shot of theirs for funny money. No wonder your average Jill can't afford a place to live around here.'

She was wearing a hoodie with sleeves that barely made it to her wrists. The material bunched around the tops of her arms like the bellows of an accordion, squeezing and relaxing to a jerky rhythm. The colour was wrong, too: United Colours of Benetton blue, its clarity dulled by age.

I had folded my cardboard coaster in half. I was staring at the crease, wondering if I could resist tearing the thing down the middle, when the screen of Alex's phone started awake.

'I'd, uh, better just have a look at this.'

Kit watched his retreating back.

'You know, he is so familiar to me, your friend. I wonder where I've seen him before?'

'Oh… he's an actor.'

'Well, you should have said something!'

'He's been in loads of things: ads and dramas and films and plays, and he does voiceovers. He did this big BBC drama about terrorists.' I nodded towards the empty seat. 'He's a slave to his phone. Never knows when he's going to get The Call.'

'It is a difficult time now, especially for you kids. Mind you, my boy Terry could never seem to catch a break, and that wasn't yesterday. I watched him grind out one application after another for jobs he had no interest in whatsoever. He had to go abroad in the end...'

She spoke slowly, her long vowels landing somewhere mid-Atlantic. I found it endearing: the rolled *r* giving way to a geetar twang.

She bleared out the window. Alex had a hand over one ear, his mobile clamped to the other. I couldn't tell from the way he was brushing his upper lip with his bottom teeth whether it was good or bad news.

'I knew he was familiar,' she said. 'Not that I watch all that much TV.' Her hand went out for her drink. 'And what is it you do, Jamie?'

'Me?'

I stared, unsure what to say, unused to having my name handed to me with such an attentive look. I told her I was an art teacher, noting the tilt of her head as she absorbed this.

'What a wonderful job.'

'It has its moments...'

'It's a vocation!'

I smiled, not wishing to disabuse her. I had become a teacher because my parents wanted me to be a teacher, and because I wanted to give them this thing they wanted as a gift or a way of atoning.

'I fell into it, to be honest.' I tapped my crushed coaster against the table, and then I said, 'A portrait painter: that's my unlived life.'

'Painting is something I have always wished I was able to do,' Kit said. 'But hey, I imagine teaching must be very rewarding.'

'Let's just say I enjoy the little moments of gratification. Like when a lesson provokes a flicker of interest in the student that I thought I'd lost forever to the view from the classroom window. That is nice. Or... or the no-work day at the end of term when they all bring in thank-you cards and boxes of biscuits...'

'You're lucky,' she said.

Lucky.

Yes, I was lucky. Most of my contemporaries had nothing: barely a job, a small fortune in debt. In between acting gigs Alex hosted pub quizzes, cleaned flats, or worked in a call centre, where he at least got to read from a script. I had sold my parents' house for around two-thirds of the amount their next-door neighbours got for theirs but compared to everyone else I knew I was up to my arse in assets.

She pulled on her beer, letting her jaw slacken to allow the maximum amount of liquid through. She kept her eyes on me.

'My sister, Annie, she's the artist in our family. Our high school teachers were always very clear with us that she was the *artiste*, and I was the scholar. I was never quite sure if that was true or if we just played along with the roles other people cast us in. You know? I remember bumping into the deputy head of the school once, years after she'd retired, and she remembered me. Well. She remembered that I was Annabel's older sister. No one ever forgot Annie! Anyway, this woman, the deputy head, told me I was looking well, and she complimented me on what I was wearing, and I told her life had been good to me, which was true, and I walked away feeling ten feet tall.'

She breathed deep, enjoying the memory. Her skin, though ruddy, looked the kind of soft I remember my mother's being towards the end.

If her eyes held mine a moment longer, I might crumple.

'The thing is,' I heard myself say. 'I've always drawn. Ever since I can remember. It's almost a compulsion. It always made me feel less... alone. Does that sound funny? Only, lately – these past few months – I haven't drawn at all. I can't seem... I can't get it together to even... Not a stroke. And I'm worried that if I don't draw, if I can't draw, then I won't... I mean, I'm worried I'll feel alone again.'

I wasn't used to talking unguardedly about myself. With anyone else, I would have stayed quiet for fear of being boring. Somehow, her eyes gave me permission. On and on I rambled, my face growing warm, and she bent her head towards me, a sign shining out from her eyes that said *I KNOW JUST WHAT YOU MEAN.*

She nodded silently.

She seemed about to say something.

*Tat. Tat. Tat.*

Alex, at the window, still with his phone clamped to his ear, pointed towards the bar, and waggled a cupped hand in front of his mouth, the universal signal for *Diet Coke.*

Kit Ross rapped the table then with just a touch too much force for that quiet corner. 'Well, I suppose I should get on,' she said. 'I promised I'd visit a friend. She's really very ill. She relies on me now, poor thing.'

She touched a hand, which was surprisingly warm, to my cheek.

'Jamie, if you need anything else, please just holler,' and off she went, the door clanging, cutting off the barman's half-hearted *Mind how you go,* and when Alex eventually came back to the table and sat down, I jolted back into the room, surprised to find that I hadn't disappeared.

He permitted himself a small shake of his head as he reached for the menu.

'What was it?'

'Voiceover for RBS: weirdly, they're not all that keen on Scottish accents now. Geordie and Brummie are the thing, apparently.'

'You should have done your Donegal. Even better.'

'Ah, but you'll come and bank with us.'

It was his mother's voice. Whenever I answered the phone to her, I had to pull up a seat to listen to the latest from her book group or the walking club while Alex rolled his eyes, his hand held out for the receiver.

'Sure, you will…'

It was uncanny.

We walked back along the track with the light softening the forest's edges. Alex was downbeat at first, but then he slipped his arm through mine, and we danced like Dorothy and the Scarecrow, a few steps side to side as the forest grew up around us.

On the doorstep we found a Tupperware box with a note: *I always go over the score. Save me from myself! KR.*

Alex prised open the lid.

'Tablet.' He pushed a chunk into his mouth.

'Well, she doesn't have to ask me twice.'

*Come in, dear children. I promise you shall eat to your hearts' desire.*

And he took another piece.

Someone, a neighbour, left a fruit loaf on the doorstep a couple of days after my mother died. When I pulled back the foil, the cake was still a little warm. I never did find out who left it there.

# Careful

My mother was quiet, but she could be bold. At fifty-something, casting around for something that wasn't the shop or us, she decided to learn to drive. Through an ad in the paper, she bought an old Fiat and talked an acquaintance into giving her lessons. She paced the flat while my father and I quizzed her on her Highway Code.

'I can't do this,' she complained. 'Why did I even get into this?'

When she passed her test first go, we all climbed into the banger, and she drove at regal pace to Portobello, where we sat on a bench eating chips out of the paper. It was a perfect evening. We watched the day dissolve itself. My mother had a gleam about her. We had been the only family we knew without a car. We went on holiday by train or coach, and once to the East Neuk in the back of a van belonging to one of Dad's friends, rattling around with the boxes from his electrical goods shop.

Mum tried to persuade my father to get behind the wheel. He made a little moue and shuddered. 'No for me.' A pal of his had been killed along with three others when the car they were gadding about in skidded into the wrong lane of the M90.

Anyway, what did he need with a car? Vans brought stock to the shop. The papers were delivered by hand. Public transport could get him everywhere he needed to go. If he learned to drive, he would end up the poor bastard giving everyone lifts everywhere.

Mum pushed back her shoulders. She was a wee woman but at times like these she seemed half a head taller than him.

For years she had talked about getting rid of her latest car, a Skoda with sixty thousand miles on the clock. It spent most of the week in the driveway. After my father died, she set about jettisoning anything that made her life difficult. It was the opposite of nesting: the great final clear out.

Often, she would stand at the window of their front room, the one kept for best, and wince at the speed of the traffic. It became almost sport, a way of raising her heart rate without taking a step outside.

I was grateful for the man who sat down with me after that long, feverish journey home. I had driven for ten hours overnight, and my mind was still shaking off the adrenal burst of Radio 1. He placed a hand on my back and steered me through the weird-smelling building, offering tea, coffee, hot chocolate, toast if I was hungry.

He looked so sad, so genuinely pained, that I wanted to say something that would lighten him. He told me my mother had lost control of the Skoda on a patch of black ice. She and the car went through a wooden fence into a ditch.

There were no other vehicles involved; the road was unusually quiet.

'The medical examiner has told us she would have died pretty much instantly,' the man said, and all I heard was *pretty much*.

The man felt compelled to offer an explanation. I heard some words about the road being dry in places and treacherous in others.

I had so many half-formed questions.

'She was unlucky,' he said.

It was that word – unlucky – that made my legs flood cold. I think I said it out loud. I felt my core tighten and the man placed a box of tissues in front of me. As I blew my nose, I glanced out of the fishbowl we were sitting in and saw the life of the police station moving around with urgency. I put my glasses back on, but it wasn't enough to block out the singing light.

'The car?'

'Was towed to a garage in...' He checked his notes. 'Loanhead of all places. Please don't worry about the car for now, Mr Haley.'

Jamie. I wanted him to call me Jamie.

He got up then and went to get me a coffee and a Snickers bar from the machine down the corridor. I ate and drank without any real awareness.

'Had your mother had any other bumps or scrapes that you know of?'

I shook my head and, when his gaze didn't shift, I wondered if I should start telling him about all the ways that my parents were careful, all throughout their lives. My mother was a steady driver who always kept her hands at ten and two on the wheel.

How else to explain her?

Perhaps I should tell him about my father's morning habit of presenting his newly shaved face for my mother to kiss? Or that they tended to bicker in the supermarket and had to divide up the shopping list to avoid further argument? Or that they went for weeks without watching television or listening to the radio because the news upset them? Or that my mother hung onto my father at parties because he was ever so slightly more socially adept than she was?

Careful People. Maybe I would have that inscribed on their gravestone. Or maybe a one-word epitaph: *Careful* as both description and warning.

I laughed into my coffee and the man looked down at his clasped hands.

'I'm afraid we'll never know precisely what happened,' he said.

But I could conjure one scenario: Mum, up to high dudgeon, checking left and right before juddering out. Maybe she caught sight of the glistening stretch, and then instead of swerving gave a panicked jam of her feet downwards, landing on the wrong pedal and sending her and the Skoda soaring.

It was one story, anyway.

My parents sometimes said that they would be happy to call it a day at three score years and ten. I didn't like that kind of talk. I wagged the finger. In the end they both made it to seventy-one, which was someone's idea of gallows humour.

My father died in August 2018, Mum in November.

*At least they're together now.*

Someone, a friend, said that to me not long after Mum died. I held onto that thought as everything moved around me in the weeks afterwards.

When I last visited, a month or so after we buried my father, she looked as pretty around the eyes as ever, and there was nothing wrong with her energy. I tried to persuade her to come and visit. 'You could come in the Easter holidays,' I said. 'It's a long time since you were down. You'd love Kew Gardens. We could go on day trips.'

'I've got those cousins in London, right enough,' she said, 'in a place called Sydenham. They came up here to stay once when I was in my teens. Sheena and Greg. We still send each other Christmas cards. Sheena thought she could sing.'

'You could take a longer trip, maybe meet up with them?'

'I'm not sure I'd be able to get away.'

'Sure, you could manage a couple of weeks.'

'You've better things to do with your time.'

'Will you at least think about it?'

'One jet setter in this family's quite enough, Jamie.'

And her chin came down against her chest: a gavel striking home.

On the train home I had allowed myself to picture the two of us catching up, sorting out each other's lives, pledging to see each other, if not regularly, at least more than we had done in recent years. Now, in my head, I was slamming a door with a sign on it saying *Jamie's Room – Keep Out*, and I was hurling myself onto my bed, covering my head with a pillow, cursing into the mattress.

My mother brushed an imaginary something off her cardigan.

'Sheena and Greg: I've no idea if I'm honest whether they're even still alive.'

The following morning, early, someone came to the house. I was lying across the sofa flicking through the *Evening News* when my mother ushered the woman through. She was ages with Mum, slight and fair-skinned with reddish hair. I didn't recognise her.

'Oh, Louie, this must be your son, is it? The teacher?'

'Jamie, this is Mrs Stone. From across the road.'

'Your mum's my financial consultant.' Mrs Stone who lived a stone's throw away raised a fat card-board folder nipped in the middle with an elastic band. 'She's been helping me with my pensions.'

'Mrs Stone's husband passed away.'

'Two years ago,' Mrs Stone said. 'And your mum's been that good to me. I don't know what I'd have done without her.' She hugged the folder to her chest. 'I'd not long moved in, and I got chatting to Louie when she was out in her garden, and she was so nice, it made me feel lucky to be here.'

Mum took her friend's coffee order. I went with her to offer help, and as I caught up with her I pressed my hand to her shoulder. Mum said nothing, just hummed a few notes to herself.

'Listen. You're all right for money and everything?'

This was vintage my parents. In a moment she would start demanding to see bank statements, tax returns, written evidence of my financial health.

'Better get going. I'll miss my train.'

We hesitated there at the door.

*Stay.* The word flashed up in my head. I wanted her to say it.

What would she say if I told her I didn't want to go back to London? I didn't want to be a teacher and live in a shoebox anymore.

Oh, she would tell me not to talk daft, the way she did when I was eight and didn't want to get all clarty at the Cub Scout Jamboree at Scone Palace.

Still, might there not be some part of her that would be pleased if I told her I didn't want to leave?

'I'll see you sometime.'

'You'll phone.'

In the hall light my mother's face looked frail. But there was such vigour in her grip when she hugged me. I swear she could have lifted me right up off the ground.

And then, on the train, my phone beeped. It was Alex. *How was your mum?* I took a moment to answer. I hadn't told her about him. He hadn't come up in the conversation. She didn't know of his existence. I had wanted to tell her about him, but how could I do justice to his height, to his brilliance? Oh, well. There was time enough for all that yet.

All the houses in my parents' row were the same: a bay window with two smaller ones just above and a roof like a blunt-cut fringe. The gardens were small but that didn't stop people from going to town, planting, sculpting the lawn, adding bird stations and tiny ponds.

Most of the driveways contained at least one outsized car. Garages were for the clutter of years. The whole estate felt cramped, the houses detached but uncomfortably close together. In distance terms it was barely a mile from where the shop had been located, but it felt a world away from the sinewy networks of the Old Town.

I spent so long planted there on the front lawn staring up at their bedroom window that a woman came out of one of the doors across the way and asked if she could help me with something. She had her phone in one hand, brandished like mace.

Mrs Stone.

'I... Jamie,' I said, pointing to my chest, as though attempting a description to a non-native speaker. When I then went on to explain, too rapidly, what had happened, the hand holding the phone went up to her mouth and she doubled over so suddenly that I feared she would fall. I ended up putting an arm around her and guiding her inside.

I opened the door to a ringing silence. Since Dad died, my quiet mother had grown to dislike silence. Sometimes she left the radio playing in the bedroom while she pottered around downstairs, as though concerned the upstairs would get lonely.

A smell of soaked fruit. Christmas cake. My mother liked to be organised. She was here, alive, only yesterday. I stumbled a little as I moved with the woman into the hallway and, for a moment, I couldn't tell which of us was holding the other up.

'Your mum was proud of you,' Mrs Stone said. 'You were following your dreams, being a teacher in London, and she always spoke of you with such pride.'

I looked down at my hands. When had I last seen her? When did we last have a conversation of more than the regulation ten minutes thrice weekly?

Mrs Stone's eyes pooled. There was a box of hankies next to the phone: the phone that brought my voice into this room. They would both sit in their chairs with the speakerphone on so they could listen at the same time.

'Oh, the way you talk, James, like you're meas-uring out every thought on a set of scales. That's Louie. You probably don't even realise you're doing it.'

The words fairly hurtled out of Mrs Stone like those strings of flowers clowns pull from their mouths.

'Even as a boy, your mum said, *He was no trouble, no trouble at all.*'

I stared past her at the photograph on the windowsill: a slender portrait of my mother with me. She's down on her heels, holding me up. I'm sporting a high collar and my light brown hair has been cut around my head with monastic severity. No longer a baby but not yet my own person. Her eyes are on me.

'When they spoke about you, they always said how lucky they were. That's how they felt about you, James. They felt lucky.'

I shut my eyes, meaning to blot out the room, and I saw my parents, undeniably old, sitting knee-to-knee on the couch, hands folded on their knees, listening to me. My mother was wearing that look she got when she watched the ice dancing: fascination mixed with a kind of astonishment. I wasn't always what they wanted me to be. I couldn't always make light.

Later, as Mrs Stone was heading for the door, wiping her eyes, throwing promises of food over her shoulder, I asked her if she knew why my mother might have taken a drive over to the other end of town so late in the afternoon.

She hesitated on the front step.

'Oh, I don't know – maybe she'd been out shopping and fancied a detour?'

'No. That can't be right.' My voice hit an uncomfortably high note. 'She always did her shopping on Monday mornings.' I moved forward as she took a step further down the path. 'No, wait.'

I checked myself, tried to sound less deranged. 'The thing is, I knew not to phone her on a Monday because *that* was her shopping day.'

'Oh, she probably took a notion. You know what she was like.'

My mother: with her aversion to unknown places and spontaneity.

Mrs Stone turned to push the front gate open; a gesture that seemed to bring her close to tears again. 'I will miss your mum,' she said.

I didn't want her to leave.


I had an impulse to see where it had happened. Without giving myself time to change my mind I ran to the Panda and drove out to the spot where she had died. It was a cold day but bright, the kind that fools you into thinking the winter isn't going to be as cruel as you'd feared. I drove along the narrow road that wound through the fields between Kirkliston and Queensferry. It was a strange thing, turning my head from side to side, trying to find something that might have taken her out there. I hitched myself up in my seat, feeling almost like I was in a thriller: the plot turning on the question of why she had been on that lonely road at that hour. As a child I had often wished to be a part of some story or adventure, but this was the kind of mystery that wouldn't end with a return to the status quo.

For a while I sat at the junction, just staring at the road running past, listening to the crescendo of the coming cars. At some point, a van hissed up behind me, and the driver blasted his horn.

'Sorry,' I mouthed into the mirror.

The vehicle chased me back onto the main road, overtaking as soon as a gap opened. 'Arsehole,' I said, my hands shaking.

I spotted a sign for a plant nursery, up ahead, and that's when I swung the car across the road and found myself entering a tunnel of trees in various states of undress. I had to circle the car park a couple of times before I found a space. Next to the garden centre a group of student types in hats with earflaps and heavy gloves were selling Christmas trees out of a portacabin. I stared for as long as was decent. My parents always left off buying their Christmas tree until the very last minute. At this most wonderful time of year, they urged restraint.

The garden centre was the usual potpourri of scented candles and birdfeed. The café was full of elderly couples and small groups, intent on their conversations and home baking. A woman handed over my coffee with a look of indifference, turning to click through the tracks on an iPod. The opening bars of Wham!'s 'Last Christmas' startled the room. There was tinsel drooping from the coffee machine and mince pies on display. I found a table by the window. Was this really where my mother had spent her Wednesday afternoons? Was the home baking worth the drive, the atmosphere so exceptional?

Growing up we rarely ate out. Coming to a garden centre café would have felt like a treat in the proper, movie-going sense.

They took me to a restaurant called The Filling Station for my tenth birthday. Mum told me I could have whatever I wanted, then added *within reason* when she saw the trouble that I was having making choices. I had never heard of a sticky toffee pudding. When the bowl arrived on the table, it contained such a brick of a portion that everyone laughed, including the staff.

'You'll never finish that,' challenged my father. Mum kept thumbing through a wad of notes in her wallet, mouthing her calculations.

The garden centre began emptying, the afternoon rush over. I looked at the clock and realised that two hours had gone by. I could feel the eyes of the woman on me as she sponged the counter. In a thriller I would show her snaps of my mother and ask if she remembered her visit. I tried to catch her attention by smiling.

'Closing in fifteen,' she said without lifting her head.

*

That night, the rain was relentless. I changed the whole shape of their living room by lighting it only with lamps. I'd made the spare room ready and warm. There was stew one of the neighbours had dropped round that I didn't feel hungry enough to eat yet.

My parents were gone. They were gone. But I would go on. I was finally settled in my mother's chair with one of my teenage Stephen Kings and I was fine. I sat back: easy in her easy chair. This was me now. This was me: alone, reading about vampires in Maine, *alone*, and I was okay.

When I awoke it was to find myself on the floor, all bent into contortions: no memory of how I got there. I stretched out my legs, sat there like a great dope for who knows how long and, when I came back into myself, I had an impulse to laugh out loud, as though there was someone nearby to share the joke.

I tried again to read. The lamps spilled triangles of light up the walls. My eyes were starting to close. I told myself: *Just move!*

As I climbed the stairs, I found myself thinking about the day we came to view this house, sixteen years ago, my father running his hand across the surface of the free-floating block the estate agent called the kitchen island, like he was afraid it might burn the ends of his fingers.

He was wearing his one and only suit because this was an important occasion.

'Isn't it just like I said?'

I thought the rooms were smaller than they had looked in the photos. People in books retired to the home of their dreams. This place was low-ceilinged, a blank. This was what they had spent their lives working towards.

It was what they could afford, was what my mother kept reminding me, especially as they had been saving up to help me out with my college.

'An ill-favoured thing, sir...' began my mother, glancing towards my father.

'But mine own!'

As we squeezed into the living room, I asked Mum if she would miss the flat.

'Oh, not really,' she said. 'It wasn't exactly what you would call a home.'

And she set her face.


Now I found the spare room that had lapsed into a drying room-cum-store cupboard. My mother had called it the Glory Hole, which made me want to put my hands over my ears and start singing. I groped for the narrow bed. I was tired and I couldn't be bothered going back downstairs for my bag, so I kicked free my shoes and slid under the covers.

The dark settled, divulging shapes. The plastic tub in the corner was full of my old books and toys. My parents were more sentimental about these things than I was. My father became so attached to certain pieces that my mother would have to disappear them into the loft: purgatory before the charity shop.

I got out of bed and rootled in one of the boxes, pulling out chipped *Star Wars* figures. Here was poor one-legged Action Man, still sporting the tank top my mum knitted for him when I complained he was cold. A mound of books: the one on top was *The Adventures of Huckleberry Finn.* The photograph on the cover was of a muddy-looking boy with great teeth dressed in overalls with a hat made of basket stuff on his head standing in front of a lake and holding up a huge fish. Corkscrew writing under the picture: *Now a Major Television Series.* I had loved that boy. I used to lie in bed and wonder why Huck Finn made my throat choke with sadness.

Right at the bottom of the box was one of my high school paintings, portentously titled *Beach After a Storm.* Landscapes were never really my thing; I had always preferred faces. I only showed my parents these creations because they seemed to lighten them. The canvas was layered with acrylic: white, turquoise, navy, black, all the darkness concentrated in one corner. I had copied it from a photograph my father had taken on a family holiday to Cornwall. The mass of retreating cloud looked like it was going to demolish the horizon. This was my mum's favourite.

Later, I found more boxes, full of pictures and things I had made dating all the way back to nursery school. Rubbish, most of it. They had kept everything.

My parents had so much stuff, all of which, Mrs Stone later reminded me, I would have to go through and decide whether to keep or throw away. Their records, books, clothes, shoes, photographs, ornaments, their gardening equipment, my mother's glasses still sitting in their case on top of the chest of drawers in their bedroom. Her glasses.

In the night, standing peeing, I spotted the sleeve of my father's dressing gown poking out from behind the bathroom door and the sight of it undid me.

Alex was shooting a public health commercial in the Lake District: he'd been cycling up and down a hill in pissing rain for two days. He'd wanted to come straight away, but I had made my voice light on the phone.

Now I battered out a text: *When you here?*

Seconds later: *Okay, I can get a lift. I'm coming.*

He was with me by lunchtime. He would be with me when I went to the hospital, the garage.

He was there when I met the undertaker and the minister. He was there of course for the funeral, dialling his smile high for all the people I had never met or even heard of and Adie Morrison and his wife and others I recognised, though now almost unrecognisable, and the couple of nervous-looking women who put a hand to their chests and said, *'Oh, you must be James!'*

And Councillor Waddell, no longer a councillor, who took my hand in both of his and said, 'How're you doing, Jamie? Anything you need. Anything at all.'

Alex stepped forward. He found for me the words that all of a sudden wouldn't form.

Mum. The easiest sound to make. Barely a word. *Mumumumum.*

There was that day I arrived home, sticky from school, to find a queue to the door and a woman looming over the counter. She had accused my mother of short-changing her. This was drivel: my mother was meticulous, but she agreed to run a till check, matching the day's receipts to the money in the drawer.

When my mother broke the news that there had been no short-changing, not on her watch, the woman erupted. Mum stood stiffly, her fingers pressed to the edge of the counter, as the queue seeped towards the door.

At some point, she sensed I was there, my mouth ajar. As the woman's voice strained higher, my mother put out a hand and gently drew me behind her, and that was enough. It was enough to coorie in, and to keep my mother between the bad things of the world and me.

As I waited for Alex to arrive, I switched on the kettle and made myself a cup of instant. Leaning on the kitchen island I had the usual view of the back garden: my father's gift to the world, dressed in its winter monochrome. When he started failing, my mum kept it alive, crowded with colour, though she disliked the cold and kneeling.

I rarely heard birdsong in London. I moved closer to the window and watched a pair of tiny sparrows (or were they finches?) singing back and forth. I put my hand to the window, gently so as not to scare them. Sparrows or finches? Male or female? My father would have known. Here on the windowsill were his binoculars, ready to be grabbed up at a moment's notice. I adjusted the focus and for a while I took solace in those sparrows or finches twitching around. I almost expected them to turn their heads and start talking to me, like the wise birds in stories. They knew everything I didn't know. Oh, they were lucky, to be so light and quick and free.

# Letter to My
# Sixteen-Year-Old Self

The heating came on with a snap, the warm pulsing through the pipes without hurry. I wore his scarf while I cooked.

'Get you something? Snifter?'

'Bit early for me,' I said.

Belatedly, I sent him a smile. To show him I was grateful: for the offer of a drink, for the week away, for him.

We fell into bed, the two of us complaining about the cold like it was a fickle friend. After we had gone back over the day, he stretched for his magazine while I lay on my side, watching him.

I asked what he was reading, and he held out the mag so I could see. The item was called *Letter to My Sixteen-Year-Old Self*. Dorien from *Birds of a Feather* smiled sagely from the page.

'You remember what you were like when you were sixteen?'

'I was a clown,' he said. 'When you're the runt of the litter you'll do pretty much anything for attention.'

'You didn't mind folk laughing at you, looking at you?'

'When I walked down Kippen Road in eyeliner and with my hair backcombed to bejesus, the neighbours shook their heads and called their kids over – the same little ass-wipes, incidentally, that threw muck at me on the way to school. My brothers pretty much disowned me.' He drew breath. 'Plus, we were the only brown people for miles around, it's not like I could escape notice. Catholics to boot!'

I hadn't thought about sixteen for so long that it only came back to me in still pictures. I remember my fascination with the boys who seemed so at home in their damp skins. Funny how the scariest boys were the ones you wanted to notice you.

'Did you know you were…?'

'Oh *yeah*. I tried not to think about it, though.'

Alex kept his eyes on me. I tried not to look away. I had grown up keeping secrets. I didn't feel like hiding from Alex.

'Whenever I had a moment alone – you know, when I was in the bath or lying in my bed – and it came back to me that I was one of *those*, it made me feel, well… you know…'

'I know.'

His mouth quirked.

'Imagine if we'd known each other, all those years ago. School. All that. We might have been friends.'

I thought about this, staring down at the covers, and when I turned back, his eyes were closed. I huddled against him until it felt safe to turn out the light.

# Art

I think I had been told to be brave, so I let go my mother's hand and joined the queue, focusing on the boy in front of me – on the straight line where his neck disappeared inside his collar. I counted to five slowly before allowing myself to look back in the direction of the gates and my mum out on the street growing smaller.

Years later, we were climbing past the school, and I heard myself telling her how much I hated it when she dropped me there. I tried to explain how bewildering I had found it, being left alone, surrounded by people I didn't know. Blurred faces, voices yelling: *Chuckle Vision, Chuckle-Chuckle Vision!*

My mother preferred to listen you out before speaking. This could be disconcerting, especially on the phone.

Her voice when it came, sounded clogged, as though she had a cold coming on.

'Sometimes I'd find excuses to leave the shop and walk past the playground when I knew you would be outside. I saw you standing by yourself, and it made me want to open the gates or climb over and just go in and take you.'

*Why didn't you?*

'I never saw you, Mum.'

'I didn't want you to see me,' she said, and then, with an edge: 'We all have to go to school, Jamie.'

I still think of big school as something I survived. I felt the change on the first day as I queued to find my name on a list and found myself buffeted in the pit of bodies reeking of wet wool and sweat. Cursing wasn't exactly a novelty: I'd had plenty of exposure to the adult world. But this was a relentless loop: *cock, shite, bugger, cunt, fuck, shite.*

The building was vast, the playground and toilets full of soft-bearded boys, holding territory. The air thrummed with constant, alert-making sound. I can hear it even now. I fled to the library, where I spent the breaks reading with my coat on. *Catcher in the Rye*, *Kidnapped*, *Lord of the Flies*. But I could never find myself in those pages.

I was there at least in the mirrors my father's glasses made whenever the light shone on them. James Haley. Boy. But not a Boy. At least, not in the way the boys in the bogs were Boys.

Outside of school I had the shop, the flat, my room: everything within easy reach. My parents' laughter and impromptu singing. At night we watched television together. My mother pulled her chair close to the box, so she didn't have to strain her eyes. My father and I sat next to each other on the couch; at times he would reach for me without a word and pull my head onto his lap.

My mother scrunched her nose at the inanity of this thing we were watching: Wogan interviewing Cilla Black and a pop star who had left his famous band and was trying to make a go of it on his own.

'Is he a poof?' my mother said. 'He looks like a poof.'

My father, without taking his eyes from the screen: 'Aye. He's a poof.'

The word struck me somewhere in the chest. A sense of shame rose in me. I had heard the word before, though I didn't know yet what it meant. It was something to do with being soft and a sook, which was how my mother described me, but it was also something to do with sex. It had come at me in the corridor from older boys, along with other words I didn't completely understand. *Jessie, queer, bufty, faggot.*

*He's a poof.* Now, I'm not even sure if this really happened in this way.

I mean I know it took place. I'm just not sure that, back then, I felt the impact of that word the way I do now when I replay the scene in my head.

It was in the library that I started to draw. At first it was a way of passing time. I spent hours copying pictures out of books, worrying at bits of faces. I filled pages with my attempts to capture Gabrielle or Damon Albarn, and then, when they were done, I would distort their features, score wrinkles into foreheads, subtly change their gender or find ways to make them ugly.

My father discovered my sketchbook. 'These are yours?' He turned the book on its side. 'Not bad. Must have taken a lot of work.'

Old Mack, the head of art, was more eloquent. I had what he called a facility. *You have a rare facility, James.* I loved the art room with its Jackson Pollocked tables, the shelves of supplies. Old Mack saw that I loved drawing, and he let me sit in the classroom during my breaks. He pinned my work on the walls. On report night, he told my parents that I should be thinking about art school.

'Oh. Well, you always were very creative, Jamie,' my mother said, and now I just have to smile. *Creative*, *sensitive*, *artistic*: the rusty words they used to explain my lack of interest in football or fighting.

They walked me home that night, deflated. Their expectation for me was that I would graduate to a professional title: doctor, lawyer or engineer, a single word they could hand customers in the shop along with their change.

'I suppose you could become an art teacher,' my father said, and that seemed to cheer them both. Mum slapped a kiss onto my head. I felt a grin creeping across my face. They were proud of me, light again.

Years later, Old Mack was sitting downstairs on the number thirty-five as I made my way to Waverley station one day. I hadn't seen him in a decade. His features had begun to blur, and his hair was feathery, but he sat upright and alert. I tried to catch his eye as I waited to get off the bus. On the pavement I knocked on the window and shouted, '*Mister Mackenzie!*' and '*Thank you!*' He narrowed his eyes and bowed his head, and I wondered if this kind of thing happened to him all the time.

There were no books in the library on how to be gay. I got the odd burst of solidarity from the conversations I read off the walls of the men's toilets in the Central Library, the safe sex ads in *Select* magazine and those films they used to have on Channel 4, the graveyard slot.

When I was fourteen, I stalked – there is no better word for it – a boy called Rich Cameron. Carmen. He'd been a few years ahead of me at school. Now he worked the counter in the post office at Waverley Gate. Between the hours of nine and five his round face stayed framed inside his individual glass window. Outside of work you saw the full glory of his sleeve tattoos and the bleached pieces in his hair just glowed.

Folk shouted at him in the street: 'All right, Carmen.' Big manly men blew him kisses. He turned around and blew them right back.

He'd taken a punch full in the face in broad daylight while waiting at a pedestrian crossing. Passing cars honked their horns in support of the lad who did it.

I dreamed about Carmen. I conjured a scene where I'd bump into him and start up a conversation that would lead to my becoming his sidekick. It wasn't sexual, not explicitly, at least not in a way I could put into words. I just wanted to be the Scully to his Mulder; or the other way round, I wasn't fussed.

On my way home from the library one Saturday, I saw him leaving the post office on his lunch break. I set off after him, keeping him just within my sights. He crossed at the lights and headed up the north side of Princes Street. Ahead of me, he stopped and looked in the window of C & A. The shop sold menswear on the ground floor with accessories in metal bins at the door.

I can still see him now: pulling out items, squirming the material between his fingers then letting the hangers swing back into place.

I walked right up to him. Stumbled at the sight of him sorting through all those shirts and pairs of trousers and pyjama bottoms. He had his back turned to me, so I stared at his neck, his tapered hairline. The solid dark layer beneath the peroxide.

When he finally turned, he barely looked in my direction. He certainly didn't show any signs of knowing who I was, whether that meant acknowledging the eager wee coupon he'd served single stamps to hundreds of times or recognising me as a kindred spirit or one of him or whatever. Carmen was used to folk staring.

All the way home I felt fleshy, short of breath, like I'd run miles. I had the feeling that everyone passing me in the street could see that something had changed, and I was wearing that change like a rosette.

I ended up back at the flat, twisting in the doorway of the living room. My father was there, watching an old film: *Now, Voyager*, with Bette Davis and Claude Rains. The film's soundtrack was overwrought and so was my father. He waved over but didn't move from his chair. He smeared the tears across his face.

Eventually, he cleared his throat and told me out of the side of his mouth that there was cold meat in the fridge if I wanted a piece.

I wanted to hide. I wanted to disappear. At school I became the Invisible Boy: a superhero with a twist, my powers triggered only when my uniform went on.

But in my year, there was a boy called Paul Duncan. He looked a picture with his yellow hair and his blush on demand. He was Prince Charming. He was the Frog Prince *after* he'd been hurled at the wall. In my memory, in the early days, he was the very definition of keen. He sat at the front of class and shot his hand into the air at every question. When he spoke, he had a stringy voice and he walked with his knees touching. For some reason he hadn't learned how to blend in, hide. It just wasn't him.

I remember being in the dinner hall one day and seeing Paul's bag flying upwards, curving through the air. Someone caught the canvas satchel, fiddled with its straps, and pitched it upwards. The teachers stood around the edges of the room. Some laughed out of the sides of their mouths.

I watched as the contents dropped out, pens and pencils, jotters, paper hankies and loose change splattering down in the middle of the room. Paul tried with all the dignity he could muster to gather everything together, but it just inflamed the laughter, the chorus of whistles.

There were tables between us. The sense of the distance I had to cover made my legs feel heavy. Of course, he couldn't see me. He pulled himself upright as he left the room, as if to say to all of us bystanders it was fine, this wasn't forever.

I remember him running a lot. Paul. Running between classes to avoid being tripped or pushed into doorways. No wonder he was skinny. I can still see that swaying crowd with Paul on the ground at the centre. He rolled onto his side and pulled his knees to his chest. The first kick went in somewhere between the base of his spine and the soft padding of his backside. I watched the whole thing from somewhere just off to the side. Or maybe I was in the air, circling. There but not there: the Invisible Boy!

His main tormentor was called Blaine. He sat behind Paul and flicked his ears, whispering insults. Blaine never once noticed me. I sat on the bench behind him in biology and stared at the penny bald spot on the back of his head.

Paul seemed mostly able to tune him out, but one day he turned, and in an instant they were both up out of their seats, grappling head-to-head, their desks leaning in like lovers. Paul's fists were full of Blaine's shirt; Blaine had his arms wrapped around Paul's waist.

The other kids were rising, slipping into a chorus of '*Fight! Fight! Fight!*' A shriek in unison from the redheaded twins Kenny and Robert as Blaine staggered into the row of desks behind.

'*Paul Duncan! Both of you. Mister McAteer's office. Now.*'

Paul shoved his desk with a vigour I hadn't seen in him for a long time and bent towards the ground. He lifted his bag as he rose, swung it wide, stretching out his other arm to slide it through the straps. But the arms didn't meet their target and the bottom of the bag slammed towards me. One of the studs caught me on the side of the head. The blow sent my glasses flying. No one saw.

'Where are your specs, Jamie?'

As I was unfolding them a crinkle of plastic broke free and dropped into my rice pudding. I had to use my spoon to fish it out.

'I wish you would try to fit in at that school.' My mother sighed as she wrapped tape around the leg.

Later – I was lying across my bed doing homework – my father knocked and put his head around the door. I could hear my mother creaking around outside, which meant there had been a discussion.

He waved from the door, his eyes roaming the room. My walls were decorated with cut outs from magazines. Almost every inch had been covered, concealed. Faces stared out from every corner. Some he would have recognised; others were too recent to fall within his frame of reference. I was trying to remember the last time he'd been in this room. Until recently the wallpaper had been baby blue, covered with dinosaurs of every imaginable species rendered in grey silhouette.

'You're okay there, are you?'

'I'm okay.'

There was so much I wanted to say to him.

'Sure?'

I felt it welling inside me.

'Yes.'

I could feel the pressure building behind my eyes. So now I had my opportunity.

'The thing is, Dad… Well, it's a little hard to say.'

And my voice cracked.

My father looked away, down at himself. His hands were resting on the headboard of the bed. When he relaxed them a moment, I could see his fingers were trembling, and I knew he couldn't stand to see me cry.

*Make light.*

So, when he looked back at me, I picked up my textbook and flipped.

'I'm fine.'

'Sure?'

'Yeah, I'm good.'

He smiled and bumped a fist off the end of the bed. He put his head back and I smiled along with him.

His eyes rose to where the wall collage was disrupted by a single, giant pencil drawing above the bed, of a chalk-faced femme fatale with nun-black beehive hair, scarlet lips curled back in a snarl.

'That's... quite something.'

'You like her?'

'Wouldn't know her if I met her in my soup.'

'Oh, she's not famous. That's Heather. From art class.'

'Never had friends that looked like that when I was at school.'

'That's my picture. I did it.'

'Not bad.'

'She's not really a friend, just someone I know from art class.'

He lingered by the door.

'We need you to keep your head down, Jamie. Your mother and me... We didn't... You know? You're a bright lad. We just need you to keep going, get to the finish line, and then you'll have... well, you'll...'

He spread his arms and they contained the world.

Mum and I took the bus up the town one afternoon, ran from shop to shop on Princes Street in the rain. We made it to the Home Stores and shook ourselves dry.

As we moved between the displays I spotted Paul Duncan on the other side of menswear, hovering next to a man and a woman I supposed were his parents. The woman was sorting through casual sweaters, pulling out items and arranging them against Paul. His father stood nearby, his arms folded across his chest.

At some point, Paul said something I couldn't hear, his face a picture of cheek. His father threw a glance in either direction, then lifted a hand and smacked Paul on the side of the head. Something leapt inside me. Paul staggered backwards, fine hair exploding in all directions. After a moment he secured his footing, swiping his hair back into place. As the flush faded a blank look settled on his face.

The sun came out as Mum and I were making our way back up the road, our arms full of bags. I spotted Paul and his parents coming towards us. His mother was tiny, bird-like with blonde hair tied back in a ponytail. The father was tall, wide-shouldered and with a gut that he carried out in front of him like a packed crate. His facial features were strong too, if evenly proportioned, not clumsily stuck on. How could such a mismatch have created something so beautiful as Paul?

They were almost upon us.

I pulled into myself, tried to become as cold and self-contained as a commie marble, but at the last moment, almost as a reflex, I looked into Paul's face, and I wanted him to see me. It was like looking into the sun.

*Blaine will go bald*, I wanted to tell him, *and that will be your revenge.*

Paul turned his head in my direction. I felt his eyes slide over mine for a second, and then the three of them passed between us, as though my mother and I were nothing but air.

'Come on, I've had enough,' Mum said. We climbed the escalator to the café on the top floor of Fraser's. There was hot chocolate with cream and marshmallows for me, and coffee and an empire biscuit for her. The windows were filled with sunlight.

'Well, look at us,' she said.

I saw her face fall and only then realised that I was crying.

I wiped a hand across my eyes.

'What is it? Jamie. Please tell me.'

'I don't know.' I looked down at my hot chocolate, the cream already seeping down the sides.

The man behind the counter had handed it over with such a flourish.

I cleared my throat a couple of times.

'I'm just so happy, Mum.'


In London, some years later, a woman stopped me in the street and said my name with an exclamation mark at the end of it. It took a while for her name to come back to me. Heather Jupp. For a moment, standing there with her shoulders sloping forward, she became that fifteen-year-old girl from art folio class again. The rest of us chewed on the ends of our pencils out of boredom. Heather chewed hers like it was made of sweeties.

She told me she'd trained as a graphic designer and had only recently moved south for work. She put her hand on my arm and asked what I was doing with my life, and when I told her I was teaching her nose wrinkled in sympathy. We reminisced for a while, our stories overlapping and sometimes conflicting, and then we swapped numbers and made plans to meet again.

When I got home, I dug out my yearbook and there she was, wide-eyed, a rabbit surprised. A few pages on, there was me, the winner of a cup for French, apparently elected a prefect and a member of the leavers' party planning committee. The theme was boy bands and girl bands.

I was laughing, thrilled by whatever the person behind the camera had said.

Paul never made it as far as the yearbook. As far as I remember he disappeared from school halfway through fifth year. I don't have a final memory of him. A while back I typed his name into Google. There were dozens of Paul Duncans but no trace that I could find of the one I wanted.

At least this way I could imagine he was somewhere in the world and that he was happy.

# Snow's Best Enjoyed in Hindsight

'Alex?'

As I scrabbled up, he raised a hand, nodding towards the wall.

'She got someone in there with her?' He was whispering.

I could hear her muttering as she padded back and forth. There was a momentary gap. I braced myself for the blurted laugh.

'Maybe she's on the phone?'

'Maybe she's guarding the family monster.'

Another pause and then a renewed guffaw so loud it made us recoil.

'Well...'

Alex put his hands over his head, his attentions moving on. His arms were knotty, his shoulders solid and strong, but there was nothing gym-made about him. He seemed naturally lithe, his skin shrink-wrapped around his frame.

I felt around for my glasses, peered at him and said good morning. Our hands and fingers made a bridge from one side of the bed to the other. He smiled and gave a little tug, and then our embrace turned into the most surreptitious fuck of all time. Alex muffled his face against my shoulder as he came. He held a hand over my mouth to stop me from laughing.

We lay there, breathing deep, and I felt something dangerously close to contentment stealing over me.

'Wait a minute,' he said. 'Listen.'

I shifted closer to the wall, shaking my head, and just at that moment there was a rap on the door, the kind that wouldn't take no for an answer. Alex slid off the end of the bed, dragging the duvet with him. He shambled across to the door, his hair sticking up at the back like a latecomer to a breakfast buffet.

A minute or two later he burst into the room, full of words.

'We're to be ready in an hour,' he said, throwing off the duvet. 'She thinks she's found your house.'

Kit was already tucked behind the wheel of her four-by-four. Alex nudged me towards the passenger seat while he folded himself into the back.

'Just shift all that junk onto the floor,' she said, sweeping away a pile of newspapers, books and a couple of travel cups. 'Well, what an adventure.'

She fired the engine. The car managed the slope in a single effortless heave.

'We almost coopered my Panda on the way in here,' I told her, glancing out the window to check the vehicle hadn't taken flight.

'You should see this place in winter. I get people coming up here for Hogmanay and I warn them about the snow and ice and then I see them toddling off to the pub in their stupid shoes and I think, well, you can't say I didn't warn you.'

'Snow's best enjoyed in hindsight. My dad used to say that.'

'Oh, I'm used to snow. Where I come from, we have feet upon feet of snow every year, much more than you get here. You have to put special tyres on your car. You wouldn't know it to look at me, but I can change a tyre in six minutes flat.'

She smiled across.

'Can you guess where I'm from?'

'Oh, I'm no good at this game.'

'I'm from Canada.' She let out a whistling sigh. 'But I'm a Scot really. In Canada, every other person will tell you they're Scottish. My parents emigrated just after the war, when my mother was already expecting me, so I'm only a Canuck by accident.' I felt myself sway as she steered us through a dip. 'Rural Ontario wasn't for me. I always knew I'd come back over here one day.'

She raised her eyes to the mirror and tried to draw Alex into the conversation.

'Hey, what do you think of the apartment?'

'Oh, it's the very dab.'

Kit gazed at him in wonder. I began listing all the things that were great about the apartment – smart, well appointed, cosy – and she grew a little taller in her seat with every superlative.

'Well, listen, I should tell the story. I'd been living in the village for a couple of years, and I saw that this place had come up for sale – it was in a terrible mess, anyone could see that, but I started to think about the possibilities. Dreaming, you know. And it sat there, unloved, and I kept coming out here, just walking around the woods and wondering.' She laughed. 'It was more like an obsession, really. Anyway, I finally phoned, and the girl who showed me around looked so... dejected, expecting nothing, and as we were leaving, I heard myself saying *I'll take it*, like I was having an out-of-body experience. Like another person's voice was coming out of my mouth. Like that girl in *The Exorcist*, you know? And when I got back in my car, I was quite pink in the face and shaking.'

Her eyes darted between Alex in the mirror and me.

'It's been a project of mine for ten years, would you believe? Scared the hell out of me at first. There were times when I thought it might never be finished, but, well, you just have to keep going forward, right? And then slowly it came together, a little bit at a time, and I thought to myself, maybe it wasn't such a daft idea after all, maybe I'm onto something here, and now – well, here we all are!'

We had come through Aumrie and were back bowling along the road Alex and I had arrived on, passing raked fields on Kit's side with the forest high up on mine. Then there was more forest, the pines arranged in regimented rows that were nothing to do with nature. The tip of the loch came into view. There was a left turn, which took us along past the picnic park we had stood in yesterday.

A few coins of rain hit the windscreen.

'It's just a spritz, don't worry.' Kit kept her eyes on the road, feeding the wheel slowly through her hands whenever we turned. 'Everything okay last night? Only I thought I heard…?'

'That would be me. Sorry, clattering around.'

Alex piped up: 'Jamie's a night owl.'

I had dinged awake at four and lain for a while, counting and recounting the days, then got up, craving the book. In the kitchen I pored over the contents page before settling on 'The Goose Girl'. I still didn't have much attention span – if anything I was getting worse; the words seemed to detach from the page and waver before my eyes – but the pale, airy illustrations told the story.

*Alas, alas, if your mother knew, her loving heart would break in two.*

I heard the line in my mum's voice.

'I can't seem to sleep past five-thirty these days,' Kit was saying. 'I thought the privilege of old age was that you had time to rest up. When Terry was going through puberty, I could never get him out of his bed before lunchtime. Everything's back to front.'

We passed a large hotel complex, the castle-like edifice set way back from the road, surrounded by lodges with pointed roofs, foothills to a mountain.

'I don't remember that being there,' I said.

'It's a few years old,' said Kit, her eyes fixed on the furthest point in the road. 'I believe they have a swimming pool and hot tubs. And a picture house!'

The road narrowed as the loch bulged, pressing the car towards the side-ditch. Kit swerved without blinking to avoid a dead something, red and mashed in the road.

*Alas, alas, if your mother knew...*

I made a feeble grab for the dashboard, my face becoming hot. I felt for the handle, and at that moment the rear-view mirror filled with Alex's profile.

'*There!*'

We said it together.

I heard myself grunt as the car swung towards a dent in the hillside. Alex was unfastening his belt, already reaching across the back seat. I could feel my heart, pulsing upwards.

The car came to a halt. Kit was looking at me.

'Do you need a moment, Jamie?'

'I'll be okay.' I looked up towards the cottage, dumped halfway up the hill. 'How did you know where to find it?'

'Oh, I have my methods.' She tried to look demure, but her face sprang back to its default setting. 'Someone around here was bound to know where your house was. I put on my deerstalker, and I asked around.'

The path went up at a steep angle. By the time we got up on the flat the sky seemed bigger than ever, blue showing through rips in the clouds.

The house was almost as I remembered – a long bungalow, built in three distinct sections, each one squatter than the last, the walls doughy in colour, so it wasn't quite the shining beacon my memory had made it out to be. The place looked to have been built back to front: no door was visible from this side, only a series of windows, the first floor-to-ceiling, with filmy drapes pulled most of the way across. Behind it, another portion of hillside got lost in trees and wispy cloud.

I climbed towards Alex and pointed at the small end window.

'That was my room,' I said. 'It was freezing and there was no central heating, but I was warm in my sleeping bag... and I had my hot water bottle...'

He pulled my hand to his mouth and kissed it then stepped away, spreading his arms, the house his gift to me.

Kit had turned towards the loch. Her head was tipped to the sky, her eyes closed. Her lips began moving, as though in prayer. As the moment stretched itself out, I became so engrossed, forgetting myself, that when she suddenly turned and looked at me I could do nothing but grin gormlessly.

'Would you like a piece of crystallised ginger?' She dug deep in her coat pockets. 'I keep it on me in case my blood sugar gets low.'

She held out her hand, with all the wrapped pieces. 'Go on, take two. They're good, they remind me of my mother. Her only vice.'

A couple of sweets slid off onto the ground.

'*Oh, Katherine!*'

I bent to retrieve them for her.

'I'm wondering if we could just have a keek...' Alex seemed about to march down the path that ran haphazard down the side of the building, weeds escaping out the cracks in the slabs.

Kit put out a hand. 'Maybe we should try knocking?'

He led the way until the path gave up, at last finding a door that opened inwards onto a glass-fronted vestibule that had at some point been bolted onto the original. Hooks bearing jackets and coats hung along the wall.

Kit cleared her throat, pointing. A woman was leaning out of the interior door, her ashen hair billowing out of a grey fleece. I saw four or five bags for life dropped around the place. The woman was almost bent double, holding the door with her rear end.

My father would have stepped in without a moment's thought. I remember one wet Friday evening standing in the rain outside the Meadowbank as he pulled a suited drunk out of a nest of bin bags. He steered the boy towards the bus stop, with me traipsing behind, handed him a pound fifty then levered him onto the bus.

'Give you a hand?'

The woman lifted her head, and I saw us suddenly: three heads crowding her doorway, and the absurdity of the image made me pull my jacket across my chest.

'Aye, well, if you wouldn't mind, son, that's good of you.'

She straightened slowly.

'You'll be all right to bring those into my kitchen, will you, son? My daughter usually goes my messages for me but she's working, and I've been staying with my younger daughter in Stirling and I've nothing in so I couldn't wait.'

'Through here?'

The smell transported me instantly to my parents' living room. I could taste the second-hand smoke on the back of my tongue.

Alex heaved his share onto the table, then stepped back and turned his eyes around the open-plan room. The kitchen area was small, crowded with too many appliances and not enough surfaces, the fridge a mosaic of novelty magnets. In the living room, there was stuff everywhere: shelves full of trinkets, pictures in silver frames, countless figurines.

The woman shuffled across the kitchen, putting out her hands to steady herself against the worktop. She reached uncertainly for the tap and poured herself a tumbler of water, knocked it back in a swift motion.

As I lifted my bags onto the table, I saw the cooker was covered in labels stuck down with tape. Each part of it was labelled: *GRILL, HOB, OVEN*, with a series of instructions etched in capitals underneath.

'My husband's got that old-timer's disease.' She pulled a packet of Superkings Blue from her pocket. 'I had to put notes on everything to stop him having accidents. He's in a home now. I looked after him for as long as I could.'

Behind me, Kit Ross spoke.

'You do what you can.'

The woman blinked in the direction of her voice.

'Here, we met before?'

'There's a good chance,' Kit said.

The woman slowly placed the cigarette in the corner of her mouth. She lit up and inhaled, seemingly unruffled by our invasion. She lifted pink-rimmed eyes to where Alex was standing, squinting along a row of knickknacks.

'You visiting from somewhere?'

'They're up from London,' Kit said.

'Aye, but where are you from, son?'

'Fintry.'

'Fintry? Scotland?' She squinted. 'Well, there was a couple staying over in Aumrie. Wee boy. I used to see them on the bus. They were from somewhere. Syrian Muslims. Nice lassie. He wasn't working.'

There was a thundering silence, which Kit stepped into.

'The reason we're here is that this young man' – I fluttered my fingers – 'remembers staying in your house when he was a wee boy.'

'Oh no, son, you've got that wrong. I never forget a face.'

Beside me, Alex breathed deep, about to launch into an explanation, then shrugged, thinking better of it, as though it was too boring to go into detail.

'It was a long time ago – twenty-five years,' Kit said. 'The house might have been a holiday let at the time?'

'Aye, well, we've been here eighteen years. Since my husband and I retired.' She contemplated me again. 'So, *you* stayed in *this* house?'

'I... Maybe.'

I turned to Alex for help. He was leaning away, trying not to get probed by her smoke.

'Aye, well, go on, then. Jog your memory.' She turned and winked at Kit, as though the two of them were complicit in some hilarious joke. 'Here, you wanting a cuppy of something?'

I joined Alex in the living room, and we stood there for a moment, pressed into the middle of the floor by the tidal wave of bric-a-brac. We opened the door outwards onto a corridor, carpeted red all the way through, with doors opening on either side. The air was cold down here, full of the same acrid smell.

Alex was in a hurry. He went straight for the door at the end of the corridor, felt the handle then pushed against something blocking the way. The room was tiny and awash with boxes, one of those breeze-block hi-fi systems, a card table with a green felt surface, the like of which I last saw in a charity shop in Camden, paperbacks spilling out of a toppled tub.

There was no clear path through to the window. Alex raised himself and tried to see the view.

'Jesus, how do I get through all this?'

I joined him in stretching and bending, making a show of squinting into corners, as though trying to find some trace of my child self. Alex was peering at the skirting board with his head bent so that his hair fell down his forehead.

'Nothing,' he said.

The door to the master bedroom was closed. Neither of us could bear to intrude, so we blundered across to the bathroom and Alex pulled on the light. The suite was mint-green and there were tiles up the walls, each one adorned with a different breed of cat. Once again, labels: *HOT TAP, COLD TAP, SINK, FLUSH.*

Alex sat down on the edge of the bath. He looked down at his thumbnail, picked at the flaking black. He seemed to be taking the state of the house personally.

We both turned our heads around the bathroom.

'I'm not even completely sure this is the right house,' I said.

And he laughed, louder than he needed to.


In the kitchen, Kit and the woman were talking.

'Yes, I heard from Shona that Christine's getting one of those camera things down her throat next week.'

'Shona will be fretting about her.'

'Oh, they'll all be frantic. I'll drop round. I'll take them something.'

Kit turned. 'Here they are, the boys. Mrs Lamont and I have just been finding out that we have quite a good number of friends in common.'

'Thank you so much for letting us have a look round,' Alex said, affecting a bow. The woman leaned to watch him leave.

Kit patted Mrs Lamont's shoulder.

'Well, I'm sure we'll be seeing each other again.'

I nodded my goodbyes from the doorway.

'Aye, well, thanks for your help, son. Like I say, my daughter usually goes my messages for me. I shouldn't be back and forth when I'm fit for the bin.'

She laughed to the end of her short breath. I knew I was meant to be going now but the colour of her face, the way she had to cling to the cooker to get her puff, kept me there, just inside the doorway.

'I'm fine, son,' she said, breathing through her front teeth, all the sass gone. 'On you go, I'll be fine in a wee minutey.'

The clouds were dispersing, the light pulling covers off the landscape. We stood around for a while in the softness of the morning. I brought out my phone to take a picture of the house. I smiled at the screen as I imagined them peering at it, their voices competing. *What's this? Now, what am I meant to be looking at here?*

I surveyed the house, trying again to make it twenty-five years younger in my head. I had a memory of sitting sketching in the hall outside the room where my parents slept, crouching close to the carpet, which I pictured now as shamrock green. I remember feeling cold and doubtful, and hoping they would wake soon, although I knew it was too early.

It had seemed a hellish journey, involving several buses, and a laden trek upwards.

'I'm not doing this again,' my father managed on the exhale. We had arrived late in the day, and the house had given us a cold welcome.

'No, don't sit down,' my mother said. 'Can we at least unpack?'

The next morning, they were able to properly take in their surroundings. My father hobbled outdoors in bare feet, clutching his binoculars. I spent hours with my sketchpad. Mum lost afternoons in a deckchair, reading her way through a pile of vicious-looking paperbacks. In the evenings we played Scrabble, and my mother laughed and shook her head when my father tried out risqué words.

We walked around the loch, stopped to eat and dabbled the water. Their movements were light. Their edges had softened.

'How old are you, Mum?' I felt the need to check.

'I'm ninety-nine,' she said, 'and next year I'll be a hundred.'

'You are *not*,' I said, and she danced away from my swiping hand.

Other than that, all I have are impressions. My father, his laughing head framed against a window. Bedtime reading made more thrilling by the novelty of the surroundings. Sliding around in my sleeping bag.

*

I turned away from the house.

At that moment, just along from us at the top of the driveway, Kit Ross was gazing out across the loch, her head back, seemingly needing nothing more than the moment.

# College

My parents were standing together at the entrance to WH Smith, bags tight against their legs, heads lowered so they wouldn't catch eyes or be forced into encounters with strangers. Whenever they dared to look up their faces seemed to lock onto the same things: a boy with a pink Mohawk, a trio of harmless Goths. Their stares moved in tandem, tracking the weird sights around the station.

Priya and I battered down the stairs and out onto the concourse, waving and shouting our apologies until they raised their heads. My father's cheeks ballooned. We shuffled into a round of greetings. I went to kiss my mother on the opposite cheek from the one she was offering, and only just avoided butting heads with her.

'Lewis's café will do us fine for lunch,' my father said.

I looked at Priya.

'Oxford Street?'

'Okay, we'll take the tube.'

My parents sagged.

'Is there not a place to eat in that M&S over there?' pleaded my mother.

'Fine.' I lifted their case, the dented brown thing that had been all over the country with us. We steered them gently across the concourse.

'How was your trip?' Priya said.

'What's that?'

'Oh, it was very nice. Very smooth,' my father said, but the look he shot at my mother was that of a frightened child.

I wriggled between them. 'I'm so glad you're here.'

The M&S café was filling up for the lunchtime rush. A circle of pushchairs formed a pen around a group of mothers and their offspring, the party sprawling across several tables. The air smelled of vanilla, coffee, second-hand crisps.

'We were lucky to get a seat,' said my father, as though we were the beneficiaries of a liberal Maître D' at the Ivy. It was September and warm, but he was wrapped up in a long, grey coat topped with handle-like epaulettes that make his shoulders cartoonishly square.

'Well, I know what I'm having, Matthew,' my mother said, lowering herself into her chair, seething at the final drop.

'I think I know what you're talking about, Louie, and I'm going to have the self-same thing,' my father said. He leaned conspiratorially towards Priya. 'They do a very good... a *very* good...'

'Cod, peas and chips, Mattie.'

Her voice ran seamlessly out of his. Looking back, this was perhaps the first time I had noticed my mother complete his thought process for him.

I went up to the counter. When I looked back my mother was staring out of the window, her hands framing her face. Becalmed, my father was now pleased to make conversation with Priya. She was smiling and answering his questions. I saw her touch a finger to her nose piercing, then her lip, in answer to a compliment or query.

Neither of them had taken off their coats and Mum's Benny from *Crossroads* hat was still pulled down around her ears. The suitcase and assorted plastic bags sat within touching distance on the floor.

I now regretted bringing Priya with me. I wanted my parents to myself. I wanted to sit and talk with them, to the exclusion of all else.

I remember the early summer of my eighteenth year as a time of giddy expectation. I felt the coming change as a kind of clenched excitement. There was talk of my parents getting rid of the shop and buying a house. I had done well. I had seen the extent of their pride when the brown envelope was opened and handed over, two pairs of glasses going on and coming off, the barrage of questions: *Now, what does this bit mean? Is that good or bad?*

A week later I watched my mother unwrap the framed copy of my results and arrange it against the living-room wall. She took a step back to admire the display. My father's smile was a mile wide. I wanted to take a picture. *I will have this forever*, I thought.

And so, I chose that moment to tell them I would be leaving.

'*London?*'

My mother turned to my father, bewildered.

My father sucked his teeth.

'You don't want to rush into anything, now.'

I felt my eyes move too quickly from her face to his. *What?*

How many times had I heard them say that the world was my oyster? Like so many Scots of their generation they measured success as being in direct proportion to the number of miles a person put between themselves and their homeland.

Was this not what they wanted?

Mum was determined to drive me. I put up a protest, telling her the train would be fine, she needn't worry, but really I was relieved. The deepening line between her brows, my father's inability to stop tugging at his watchstrap, would help distract from my own fears. We would travel down slowly, stopping off in the Lake District for a few days, and it would feel more like a holiday than a leaving.

They tried to stay upbeat, all the while letting drop warnings about how difficult and expensive my life would be. They looked at me appalled when I told them I would be getting a weekend job. ('But what about college? Your studies?') My father hurried to the living room table, pulled out scraps of paper and began adding the cost of my accommodation to the tuition fees before deducting the paltry scholarship grant.

I saw my father wince. He may even have put a hand to his mouth. And this was even before they had factored in the exorbitant bus or train fare home.

'Let me see that.'

My mother started again on a fresh sheet of paper.

The numbers were the same.

Yes, she conceded, I would have to get a job.

The train fare home, the booby prize on *Bullseye*: that was the thing they kept coming back to, as though that word – home – would keep burrowing into me until I changed my mind. But home wouldn't be home anymore. The Purple Shop was on the market, and they had settled for the house in the huddled row with the low ceilings and featureless walls. I tried to think of that house as home. Whenever I thought of it, I had to hold my breath against the memory of the newly laid carpet.

A day or two before I was due to leave, my father took me aside and told me said fare would be covered, whenever and as many times as I chose to come home.

Home.

It would have been easier to give in, admit they had a point and settle for Edinburgh, where I had never fit in, but where at least I could live rent-free.

But I dug in. I don't know where it came from, this resolve. Where I usually walked around with my eyes on the ground, I now straightened my back, partly to reassure them and partly to dupe myself into believing I wasn't scared.

In the Lake District we forgot ourselves and the mood was light. We gave nicknames to the people we saw regularly at the hotel and made up stories about them. We walked for miles and stopped in at cafés and talked about things from the past.

My mother began every other sentence with, 'Do you mind the time when…?' and my father leaned over the table and countered, 'No, that's not right, is it…?'

At times he laughed so hard I had to pat his back and ask him to repeat what he'd just said. They complained about the ways Edinburgh had changed, remembering grand buildings and colony houses that had been torn down and built up again, of glass and steel this time. They talked about the shop in the past tense.

They were keen to buy things, practical bits for me like a toaster and blankets as well as postcards and mementoes. As we were leaving the hotel on the last day my father stuffed a twenty-pound note into my jacket pocket.

'Remember to eat,' my mother said, and she looked at me sideways, checking she wasn't talking to herself.

A change came over them when we arrived in the student village. Between the foyer and the third floor of that unprepossessing concrete block, I sensed them gathering in their concern, becoming self-possessed, poised. There were people my age everywhere, with the same stiff resolve: trying not to look like they were wetting themselves. The three of us had to squeeze into the single room with the sink in the corner and the desk by the window. I tried not to look at their faces, but I imagined an air of calm settling in the room, even if they were inwardly sad and worried.

I said a polite no thanks to their offer to help me unpack.

'I'm fine,' I said, but I was lying.

My father sat on the bed. As I waited against one narrow wall, a boy poked his head through the doorway, grey eyes beneath the first shoots of an Afro.

'Hey. Jasper. Across the way.'

Bravado carried him through the door. He offered a hand, his skin a little cool to the touch. My father shuddered to his feet. I tried not to smile too eagerly at my new neighbour. 'Jamie.'

'Oh! Whereabouts in Scotland are you from?'

'We'll just get going, then,' my mother said.

She was already standing by the door.

There was a loose embrace, during which my father produced a biro that ended up in my top pocket. 'In case you need to make notes.' They backed up, turned and clipped along the corridor, and I returned to Jasper with an ache at the base of my skull.

There was a lot of clinging in those first weeks. I held on to Jasper through the principal's address. When term started, I stood at the edge of a group I hadn't been invited to join until I finally forced myself to say something. Gradually we formed one large circle and took it in turns to speak into the terrifying gaps. I almost shouted to make myself heard. We laughed at every glib comment. We remarked on each other's clothes and accessories. There were a lot of questions for me about Scotland and Edinburgh. Did I hate the English? And what were Highers anyway?

When it came to the formal introductions we listened as our classmates set out their stalls, all the while churning silently through our own achievements, dismissing them as pathetic, vowing to do better, work our socks off, make progress.

We sat and drank coffee and smoked in the college bars and around the massive tables in the central lounge of the student residence.

The conversation went from surface to deep in the space of one short toke.

'So, who's out here?' said a girl with a skullcap of black hair, her hand in the air. A couple more hands went up. 'I'm bi,' said one boy, with half a hand up.

I held my mug in front of my face, unsure at first what they were talking about. I realised after a moment that every eye was on me.

*Is he a poof?*

*He looks like a poof.*

Slowly, I raised a hand. Priya, who had asked the question, leaned forward and smiled, as if to say: 'See, that wasn't so difficult, now, was it?'

And the realisation went through me like a fright. *It was easy.* I took a breath, filled my lungs, as though I was miles out in the countryside instead of a stuffy student lounge. I lifted my chin. I wanted to throw both my hands in the air.

*Je suis un pédé!*

*

It hadn't occurred to me that there could be so many out people in the world. I was fearful at first, watching Priya and the others, not sure how to be. It took me a long time to get my bearings. Our crowd went to a club called Generator and I stood at Priya's shoulder while she picked out boys for me.

There were boys in print blouses and girls in bow ties and braces and then there were the ones who were neither boy nor girl and I stared, amazed at how lightly they carried themselves.

Someone with points of silver hair and blue above their eyes came over and stood smiling, holding out his or her hand. As we moved off together, this beautiful creature and me, I could see Priya waving as she leaned against the wall with her beer. She waved across the sea of heads as the silver-haired one danced me out of sight. I closed my eyes, finding my rhythm.

Priya and the rest, these were the friends I would carry with me through the next years. They saw something in me. Priya drew me out with her warmth and attentive face, and she shared something of her own past life, though it was difficult for her to talk about the parents who had pretty much disowned her for wanting something they didn't want for her.

She radiated calm but I could see her anger in the way her lips tightened when she lit a joint. She had two younger sisters, still at home. She hoped to see them again one day.

We marched against Section 28. We manned stalls and sold whistles and badges for civil partnerships and equal marriage. We were activists. Down Park Lane we marched, round past Hyde Park Corner, along Piccadilly and onto Trafalgar Square and Whitehall, banners flapping; it got to the point where we could have walked the route blindfolded.

When I called my parents from the payphone in that mud-coloured corridor I pictured my father in the front room of the new house, studying the receiver, twisting it around its cord until it was the right way round. I imagined him holding up the phone so my mother could listen. I heard two sets of smoker's breath shuddering down the line.

They wanted to know all about my course. Was I working hard? I told them I was thinking about getting another job in one of the bars on campus.

'Look, if you're short of money, I could maybe send you a bitty extra,' pleaded my father. 'Train fare home,' he said, in Jim Bowen's Lancashire accent.

I can't know what life was really like for them when I wasn't there.

A bundle of my housemates went past on their way to college. 'Where are you speaking from?' my mother said, hearing their chatter.

'You sound a bit funny,' my father said. 'What's happened to your voice?'

'*Matthew.*'

'Sounds like he's sucking on soor plooms,' I heard my father say.

In a moment of afterglow, I told my parents that I had been on a march around campus, protesting cuts to higher education funding and student finance. I didn't tell them that the organisers had burned an effigy of Charles Clarke.

There was a silence, and then my mother said, 'We don't want you getting involved in any of that stuff. You just keep your head down, Jamie.'

At Christmas I showed them photos of the work I'd made that term.

'What am I looking at here?' my father said. They were looking at an entirely blue room peopled with action figures, all of them painted blue, with one tiny circle of white high up on one wall. 'It's meant to represent inequality,' I said.

Dad burst into laughter. My mother placed a hand on his arm.

'We prefer your drawings and paintings, Jamie,' she said.

Now we emerged into daylight, Priya and I walking slightly ahead of my parents.

'Are you okay?' she said. 'You're not yourself.'

It was true: I had toned myself down. That morning I had stood in front of the bathroom mirror and tried to remember what I looked like six months earlier, a year earlier. So, I was wearing navy and I had put on my glasses and tamed my hair.

Outside the station I spotted a gap in the traffic and pushed across the road, doing that London thing I had learned of weaving with faked confidence between slow-moving traffic just as the lights changed. We made it onto the opposite pavement just as a convoy of buses and taxis started swinging around the corner and turned to see my parents still waiting on the other side of the road.

They stood elbow-to-elbow, faces curdling at the height and speed and volume of the traffic.

A heartfelt *fucking hell* from Priya. Her mouth opened as my father dipped a tentative toe, then stumbled back as a bicycle streaked past.

We raised our hands, fingers spread and mouthed at them to wait.

They couldn't check into their hotel for another couple of hours, so I invited them back to the flat. We lived in Brixton by then, another long ride from the centre. We couldn't talk much because of the noise the tube made between stations, so we just sat really close together, me with my arms around their suitcase, staring ahead between the roof and the floor. When I looked up at my mother, she was hanging off one of the eye-level handles with her eyes closed.

In our block the stair light was out. My dad had to stop for a breather on the steps. Mum placed a hand on his back. At the top, Priya spread her arms in welcome, then retreated to her room, and I guided my parents across the hallway and into the kitchen where my mother eased my father into a chair.

I saw them taking in their surroundings, nodding their heads, and glancing at each other. This was not what they had been expecting. I saw that now. There were still breakfast and lunch dishes stacked along the surfaces and a plastic box in the corner overflowing with empty cans and bottles. Homemade banners, pictures of Meg from The White Stripes at her drumkit and Kelis and Cat Power, and posters for *Oldboy* and *Ghost World* covered the walls.

The windows were wide to the world to get rid of the smell of grass. I had spent the best part of the previous day cleaning but my parents' idea of house-proud was different to mine.

My father slowly pulled his feet free from the linoleum. Perhaps it had been a mistake to bring them here.

I would atone. Tomorrow, I would take them on one of those open-topped bus tours. We would make excursions to Kew Gardens and Hampton Court Palace. I would let them see the London they wanted.

My mother bared her teeth.

'You said you were going to show us some of your drawings, Jamie.'

I escaped to my room, ran back with my portfolio, worried that something might happen while I was gone – someone might walk through in their skimpies or perhaps the pulley bearing a week's worth of six people's washing would come crashing down on their heads.

They had both taken off their coats and were standing at the sink. Mum was making her way through the pile while my father at her side did the drying. The dishtowel was a souvenir from a Pride stall, covered in slogans: *Keep Calm and Wear a Condom* and *Just Cover Your Willy, Silly.* Maybe my father hadn't noticed.

Later, as they got ready to leave for their hotel, I caught a glimpse of them in the mirror through the open door of the bathroom. My mother was worrying at her hair, patting, and pulling at the fringe as though trying to stretch it. She squinted at herself, wiped at an imagined smudge of her eye pencil. As I watched, my father came up behind her, placed both hands on her shoulders and put his face on her shoulder, then looked up. I could feel the warm of his breath against my own cheek.

My mother put her hands over his and they smiled at each other in the mirror. I wanted to squeeze between them. I wanted to put my face between theirs.

# Stay

We lit lamps and I made tall sandwiches and Alex hunted through the cabinet under the TV for entertainment. He discounted Rummikub and Cluedo before settling on an antique edition of Guess Who?

He stared at the rows of cherub faces.

'No wonder I grew up with an identity crisis,' he said.

We ate to a soundtrack of clicking tiles and an insistent rhythm from next door. Alex raised himself by the elbow. 'Is she listening to Grace Jones?'

I dragged a blanket from the sofa and wrapped it around my shoulders. Alex pulled his board onto his lap.

'Robert reminds me of my ex,' he said, mimicking the depressed little face.

We lay together on the floor, playing Capping Exes where I told him about Gareth, who wet his hair every night before bed to keep it soft. He told me about a boyfriend of his from college who would lie perfectly still on his back during sex and insisted on coming into a paper hanky. I told him about Roger, who couldn't get it up until he'd enjoyed at least twenty minutes of porn.

I ran out of stories, but he kept his eyes on me, expecting more. Instinctively, I made to sit up, pulling the blanket tighter, but he put his hand out. *Stay.*

He took my hand, held it, and as I looked into his searching eyes, I began telling him something I had never told anyone else, about what happened with Councillor Waddell the summer I was fifteen.

There had been the usual gathering in the flat and I had shown face. My parents had insisted I make an appearance, even if it was only for ten minutes. I was fifteen – I had other priorities.

They were talking to Councillor Waddell. As I shuffled over to join them, he turned and sighed a lungful of smoke out of one side of his mouth.

'The councillor was just saying he's on the board of a couple of galleries in the New Town,' my mother told me. 'He might be able to get you a summer job.'

'I can look into it for you,' he said. 'If that fits in with your plans, Jamie?'

My plans had been to work in the shop, sit in my room reading and perhaps try to capture Leonardo DiCaprio in my sketchpad.

'That would be great.'

'Thank you, Councillor Waddell,' my father said.

'Thank you, Councillor Waddell,' I said.

'Adrian, please,' said the councillor.

He smiled at each of us before moving on to another group.

As I sat with my parents, wondering when I could excuse myself, I sensed him looking over at me. I still thought he was good-looking, in a thin-faced, tired-in-the-eyes kind of way. I smiled at him then looked away, daring myself to look back, realising with a cold rush that his attention was still on me.

I muttered the word homework and went out and stood for a moment in the hallway. Behind me the door to the living room opened and I felt my heart thudding against the inside of my chest as I turned around and assumed the face that I reserved for teachers who sought me out for grown-up conversation: attentive, flattered.

'So, you're keen on art, are you, Jamie?'

'And English. And French.'

I tried to think of something to say that didn't sound like a shopping list, at that moment realising how close his face was to mine. His breath was fresh with the beer, not unpleasant.

I lifted my face, but he was hesitant, and in that startling silence I tried to get a sense of what was happening. Seeing him watching me from the other side of the living room, I had thought I wanted something from him. I was ready for this, I thought. I was ready. Now, I realised, I didn't know what I wanted, and it was thrilling.

Someone had to make a move.

When he put his hand out to take mine it was shaking. He held the ends of my fingers and, when I didn't move or resist, he sighed, the lower part of his face trembling. For a moment he looked like he was going to cry. I looked down, wondering what my clammy palm felt like in his.

He started telling me how lucky I was to be young with so much going for me. He told me I deserved all the luck in the world. I was lucky. The words came in a rush, like he was scared some ghoul might creep in and break his train of thought.

And then the tears dropped from his eyes and shattered on the floor. His shoulders were heaving. This wasn't what I was expecting.

I'm still not sure what came first: me sliding my hand free, touching it to his elbow, a tentative offer of comfort, or the sound of the living room door opening, which he obviously heard before I did. I froze on the spot – my face must have been a picture – but Councillor Waddell took a step back while drawing himself up to his full height, palming away the tears, feeling in his jacket pocket for his fags, pulling himself together in a moment.

It was my father.

'Not bending your ear, is he, Councillor?'

'Homework,' I said.

I sidled along the wall, backed towards my room, hot in the face, relieved, sad and murderous with loss.

Outside the door, I could hear Councillor Waddell making his excuses. *My wife*, he was saying, comically, as though the quiet, smiling woman who sometimes accompanied him on his rounds were the punch line to a joke.

Alex worked his mouth a couple of times.

'And what do you think he would've done if your dad hadn't appeared?'

'I'm not even sure he would have done anything.'

'And you didn't tell your parents?'

'Would you have told your parents?'

Alex thought for a moment.

'Maybe,' he said, smiling, so I didn't know if he was joking or not.

I wouldn't have told. At fifteen, I was made of secrets.

# Work

When my graduation came around, my parents took the train down for only the second time since I had moved away. They dressed in their summer smart clothes and took photographs. My dad swung his cup of elderflower around and spoke to the lecturers like they were his comrades from the folk club. My mother's smile was shy and lovely. I was happy for them.

My scroll was taken from me and placed in my mum's bag. It would be unrolled, framed and hung on the usual wall.

After we graduated, my friends and I were not short of plans. We sat around and talked and drank and got stoned. We got it together enough to organise a group show in a gallery in Walthamstow. The owner was looking to get the word out and said he would give us a discount.

I was offered a corner of the big white space in which to display my charcoal portraits. We arrived early to set up and get tucked into the free cider we'd blagged as sponsorship in kind. It was a glorious evening and so the gathering lurched out onto the pavement. My friends looked more beautiful than I'd ever seen them look before. We all danced and roared along to 'You Make Me Feel Like a Natural Woman'. We were overexcited, and so world-weary.

When it grew chilly, we spilled back inside, remembering why we were there, sniggering at the mixed bag of nuts that was our so-called exhibition.

I phoned home.

'I sold two pictures,' I said.

'How much did you get for them?' ventured my mother.

It amounted to a month's rent, but it sounded like nothing when I said it out loud.

'Good for you,' my father said, and I wished I had just lied.

Through the same gallery I made some more sales, and my large-canvas portraits were included in a group show in Hoxton. For a while, I was having fun, everything seemed possible, but not long after, when I looked at my life with a cold eye, I realised how broke I was, how tired and out of shape I felt.

What artist makes a living in London? I took on extra work as a waiter and liked the cold money. I still drew, mainly sketches of friends, which I sold for the price of a coffee and a piece of cake or gave away as gifts. I noticed how many of my classmates were moving on, studying again or retraining. Some were finding jobs in the City. Overnight, they began walking around in clothes that didn't come from vintage shops and with proper haircuts.

Sell-outs, Priya called them, and I harrumphed along with her.

To keep going you need money. So, there were more cafés and restaurants, evening shifts in offices, punching numbers into keyboards from six-to-ten. For a time, I went with my office colleagues to their pubs after work. These guys lived for the Friday night binge. I stuck around for as long as I could: went home when the collars and tongues got loose. *You're gay, right? My gay friends are a blast; they're the life and soul.* While they waited expectantly, I grinned like a clown. Gurned until my face hurt.

I was fine, I told myself. I was self-contained. I was in *London*, for god's sake.

When I could I took myself off to preview nights at the theatre. Sat in the stalls, soaking up whatever bodily warmth the person in the next seat gave off. I took trips to the National Gallery with Priya. We ascended to the Impressionists and lost ourselves in coloured dots. I read everything I could lay my hands on, from charity-shop classics to the trash people left lying around at work, or I buried myself in the screen of my laptop. I became addicted to certain porn sites, attaching to my most beloved adult performers so completely that I began to think of them as friends.

I travelled across town on the tube for hookups, marvelling at the wee nooks my dates could squeeze themselves into while they told me, proudly, how much they were paying in rent.

*An ill-favoured thing, sir...*

I began to wonder if I might one day be able to afford to buy a shoebox of my very own.

I started canvasses then abandoned them. I mislaid my sketchbook and made a half-hearted search. I devoted my creative energies to carving hearts in froth and garnishing pies. The rest of it – art, ambition – wafted away.

I stopped looking for my sketchbook.


I was twenty-three. The flat I'd been sharing with friends was sold. We looked around, Priya and I, but couldn't find anything within our means that wasn't derelict. I embarked on a career of couch surfing, everything I needed stuffed into one bag.


'How are you doing?' my parents asked.

I was calling from my mobile, using free minutes because I didn't have access to a house phone anymore.

I did not say: *I can't keep my feet moving underneath me. There's too much of this London. I have almost forgotten how people talk to each other outside of work.* I painted a portrait of myself that I knew would please them. Over time my lies grew limbs.

I was selling paintings, I told them, getting commissions. I had a lovely flat in Paddington (where the couch I was residing on happened to be). I had turned my spare room – *a spare room! In London!* – into a studio.

'Well, I'm assuming this means you won't be coming home to see us any time soon,' my father said.

I put the phone down, becoming me again, wracked with worries. I wanted to lie down. I took out a pen and paper and totted up how much money I had to keep me going until the end of the month. It was a hobby now, a compulsion.

Whenever I asked on the phone how my father was doing my mother would say, 'Oh, much the same,' before steering me elsewhere. I didn't argue, though I knew that home was work for my mother now. My role as ever was to make light, on the phone or in letters: conjure up a world of arty high jinks she could escape into whenever things became too difficult.

When I did go home, which wasn't often, I saw that my dad was still reasonably lucid: taking longer than usual to immerse the teabag into the cup and add the boiled water, but most of the way to who he had been.

There was one visit, a couple of summers after I graduated, when I sat listening to him talk on a loop about his new interest in holiday programmes and how he was planning to persuade Mum to go somewhere warm for a change. I leaned closer because his voice already sounded far away.

'Your mother could do with a break,' he said.

I tried to conjure the pair of them on a beach somewhere, wearing too many layers, cramped, complaining about the temperature. *It's just a bit too hot...*

I was twenty-four and I had succeeded in splitting myself. There was the messy Jamie, stumbling from one job to another, sleeping like a teenager on my days off, and the version I had tried selling to my parents.

My friends drifted; the group diminished. I told Priya I was done with this life of cafés and offices. I would work for myself. I would paint full time.

'Hell, yeah!' she cried, making pistol fingers.

Maybe I would go back to college and learn a new skill. After watching a programme about posh plumbers, I imagined training up, starting my own lucrative business.

But then I would feel the envelope of wages lumped in my hand and it seemed I had fuel for another week and that was enough for now.

On my twenty-fifth birthday I was flat-sitting for a friend of a friend in Vauxhall, not far from my latest café. The flat was large with a balcony that offered a splinter-view of the river.

One evening I left work with my co-worker Danny, who was seven years younger than me with long braids. Who talked nonstop, not caring to disguise his sibilant S; who moved through life like a gentle breeze. We bumped up the street, our shoulders touching.

Neither of us noticed the guy until he was almost upon us. He was stomping the pavement with such heavy momentum that there was nothing Danny and I could do when he reached us but pull apart. I said nothing – it hadn't occurred to me to respond – but Danny swept round, braids lashing the air: *Excusez-moi!*

The man turned like a piece of heavy machinery.

His voice was a surprise: high-pitched and nasal.

*You two stab each other's arses!*

Not from here, a northerner. Scouse or Mancunian.

He moved forward, lower lip protruding.

*Arse-stabbers!*

I moved off, pulling Danny by the hand, but Danny wasn't done. He flicked the Vs.

The man was on the move. We were running now, Danny in peals of laughter. As we reached my building I grasped my keys, pushed Danny inside, and just at that moment we heard the rush of feet like a sudden rainstorm.

*I'm going to fuck you, arse-stabbers. I'm going to fuck you up the arse. You fuckers. You arse-lickers.*

Between us, we managed to push the door. Danny hammered numbers into his phone while I held it closed. The man shouldered the door until my weight gave way.

*I'll huff and I'll puff...*

I fluttered backwards, and he was suddenly there in the foyer, lagging by the door.

Then – *Fuck, arse, fuck* – the hate all started up again. I had a quick look behind me, towards Danny, the stairs, and just then the man lunged, and I put my arms up, shot out a hand, the flat of my palm catching him on the shoulder. Danny shouted; I turned to run, but the man was on me then, rugby tackling me around the waist. I lost my footing, becoming disorientated. Everything slowed. I was fourteen again, back in the playground. I was Paul Duncan, bracing for the first punch or kick.

*I'll blow your house down!*

He picked me up like a bag of rubbish and threw me away. I sat up, and there was a moment then when I looked him square on and saw his stiff, black eyelashes, and childlike hesitation. Maybe I wasn't done for.

*You don't have to do this*, I started to say, but the sound of my voice only provoked him.

Once, twice, three times, I felt my shoulders slam against the wall.

A jumble of voices. Danny had run into the street for help. I felt myself sway forward into silence as the man took off running.

Alex tightened his grip on my hand.

I called in sick to work, sat in my room in the flat that wasn't mine and watched films. I caught the pictures on the news of the pope arriving in Edinburgh. The city looked pretty, and the sun was shining for once. I took out my phone and dialled my parents' number and got their new answerphone. I smiled at the time it took for my mother's voice to come on the line. She had softened her accent, rounding the vowels the way she thought people were meant to talk on the telephone. I sat in my room in that beautiful flat and stared down at my phone, willing it to come awake.

I couldn't afford the train, so I took the Megabus. My head kept sinking onto the shoulder of the woman sitting next to me. When I arrived at the bus station in the evening, I went into the toilets and changed my shirt and socks, combed my hair, and brushed my teeth, cleaned my specs, sprayed deodorant, every corner tucked in.

Mum was inching along Queen Street in the car, neck craning. Her face, washed gold by the street-light, contorted as she heaved the wheel. 'Traffic's terrible.' Then, an acknowledgement I was there. 'Did you have a good trip?'

As the car strove upwards, squeezing between all the parked cars in their crowded estate I got my voice ready, mouthing the words 'Hello' and 'How are you?' and stretching my face wide like I would for any other visit.

Mum slotted the car home.

'Well, I'd better get inside and check on your father.'

But she didn't move. She sat for a few moments before unbuckling her belt.

'It's good that you're here,' she said. 'Gives us all a wee shot in the arm.'

For tea, she'd made a lasagne. The appearance of any dish with a three-syllable name meant a special occasion. When she put the plate on the table my father just smiled at it. After a moment she got up and began cutting his slice into ever-smaller pieces.

When my father didn't respond she forked one of the chunks, then put the implement in his hand. He held up the fork, turned it around, smiling.

I looked down at my plate.

'You want a... drink of something?' she said.

She hurried over the word *drink* in the way some people flinch from the words *hospital* or *operation*.

'You can have orange squash or... I think there's fizzy in the cupboard: blackcurrant and... something.'

'Water's fine.'


My father went to bed around eight thirty. My mother went with him, signalling for me to stay put. I hovered around the living room, listening to the creaking from upstairs. I was sighing a lot, as though there was a shortage of air in the room.


Later, I watched Mum counting through her pack of Regal, taking out that evening's cigarette, her one and only of the day, which she would now smoke standing at the back door, looking out into the darkness.

I heard her pacing the patio. When she came back in, the tension ebbing, she told me she was going to make a tea. She had her back turned to me as she rattled the jar and mugs with more vigour than I had seen her use before.

And then I began. I had practised by rote, but when my mother didn't say anything, I kept going, making strings of words, out-of-body, as though this was happening to someone else.

She lifted her mug, pushed her hair out of her face.

'Are you hearing me, Mum?'

She whirred her spoon in her tea.

'But what about Priya?' she said.

'Priya?'

'That girl – her name was Priya, wasn't it? The Indian girl.'

When she turned, I saw she had this look of forlorn hope. There was a beat and then I burst into laughter – *Priya?* – which turned out to be absolutely the wrong thing to do. My mother slammed her cup down, slopping herbal infusion over the counter.

'Your life will be *hard*. You'll be lonely. People will laugh at you.'

'Look, I won't say anything to Dad if you don't want me to.'

For a moment her face seemed to break.

'Oh, I suppose he knows.'


The next day I watched my parents go through the many slow rituals that made up their life now. My mother went from one task to another without a sigh, but I could see she was angry. She could barely look at me.

I knew what to do. I would train to be an art teacher. I would give her this thing she wanted, I would work hard at it, and perhaps this would give her the shot in the arm she needed.

I was twenty-six. Home on another visit, I woke to voices, the radio at full blast. My father was sitting at the head of the kitchen table, staring hard at something in his paper. He'd been up since half six, he said. A cup of hot water and a quick dook under the shower followed by a walk to the shop for the milk and what he still called his comic, then home to spread the pages out in front of him.

This was romance: the paper came through the letterbox every morning. The pages were so long and wide that sometimes he had to stand up to look at the topmost articles.

He stared at me. 'Did you sleep well?' All weekend he had spoken to me like a hotel guest. 'There's orange juice,' he said. 'We have the one you like, the green carton, without the wee bits.'

The orange juice seemed significant: it was a detail he had remembered about me: *Jamie doesn't like freshly squeezed orange juice with bits of fruit that float about in the liquid and feel funny in your mouth when you take your last gulp.* I was touched, even though I had last made that complaint about the orange juice when I was nine.

'Thanks, Dad.'

The newspaper crackled.

I sat down and asked him what was in the news. He sighed, launching into a familiar rant about David Cameron, what a con artist he was, his latest attempt to ingratiate himself with Labour folk. Dad could be so lucid when you got him onto the right subject. As he rattled on, I was trying to wrench something out of him with my eyes, some recognition, some further sign he knew who I was, what tied me to him. I wanted him to tell me something I didn't know. More than anything I wanted him to tell me about the day I was born, twenty-six years ago. Was he, my father, there? What did he think when he first saw me? What was I like as a baby? Did I give him and Mum much trouble?

And I wanted him to smile and put his hand in my hair like he was fond of me and tell me no, I was gorgeous and no trouble. Good as gold.

# Rumpelstiltskin

I told Alex stories until I felt light-headed, dried. He sat with his back against the sofa, arms across his body, legs out in front of him, as though straitjacketed.

'It's hard for me to... I don't always remember...'

I broke off and drew outlines in the air.

He asked what I wanted to do the next day.

'Let's drive somewhere. We could drop by and see your mum.'

'Great. I'll take myself out for a long walk while you two catch up.'

He stretched out across the floor and felt for his phone.

'Oh.' He sat up. 'You mind that radio series? Radio documentary series: Scotland's gin-making phenomenon. You remember? I've got a call-back.' He scrolled. 'Oh, for fucksake...'

'What?'

'It's tomorrow. Okay, I'll leave it.'

He continued to stare at the screen, his mouth turning down at the corners.

'Come on,' I said. 'You can be up and back in a day.'

'Dunno.'

'I'll be fine.'

He raised himself. 'You're sure?'

'Hey, this is good news.'

I pressed my hand into his, jiggled his fingers to show him how fine and how light I was.

'Okay, then. Right.'

'You've got this.'

'I mean, I could do this standing on my head, right?'

'Bed then, mister!'

'Yep.'

*But what will I do tomorrow? What will I do with all those hours?*

Alex really did sleep like a child: open-mouthed, chest heaving. It was quite something to see, almost parodic. I watched him in silence, nothing to mar the moment.

Still, I had to get up and feel through the dark for my book.

I used to be so scared of *Rumpelstiltskin*; the people in the pictures stick-like, long-headed, like Giacometti sculptures. Their faces are smudged:

all the dwarf's rage is in his clenched fists and stamping foot.

Now I made myself look, the old fears solidifying again.

When my eyes began to hurt, I went to the kitchen window and fumbled with the handle so I could drink the breeze. I leaned into the night.

I almost didn't notice the first sounds of movement from next door. Was it that time already? I went over to the wall.

*Hello.* If I knocked, would she knock back? Maybe we could develop a whole way of communicating made up only of knocks.

'Well, what do you think?'

Alex opened his palms then slapped them to his sides. He wasn't wearing either of the outfits we'd mulled over earlier. Instead, he'd put on a white round-collared shirt and black jeans.

'A neutral canvas.'

'Perfect for radio.'

He fisted his hands, landed a mock blow against my chin. He was smiling but his nerves showed in his pacing and sighing. It's only me who sees this.

He lifted his messenger bag and threw it over his shoulder.

'You'll phone?'

'Soon as I'm done.'

He yanked open the door. And there in the frame was Kit Ross; pink from activity, with a jumbo carton of orange juice tucked under one of her arms.

'You look like you're off out somewhere.'

'Only to Glasgow.'

'An acting job!'

'I'm leaving this one holding the fort.'

Alex half-turned and squeezed my shoulder.

'Break a leg,' Kit said, beaming.

A half-arsed honk of the horn as he moved off. Kit and I winced in harmony as he failed to take the slope at the first attempt and rolled backwards for another try.

A victory blast as he got to the top, and then the car lumbered out of sight.

'What an exciting life you boys lead,' Kit said.

Slowly, I took off my glasses, pretended to clean them on my sleeve.

I had remembered that the boot of the car contained the cardboard box with the taped-down lid I had brought from my parents' house. I had gathered Fotheringay and Fairport Convention, Pentangle and the Humblebums. An old cash box I'd had for years, with some of my doodles inside, letters and my birth certificate, snaps of my mum and dad and pictures of me when I was a kid. A couple of primary school sculptures made of papier-mâché, toilet roll and crepe paper. They were all there, in the car, bound for Glasgow.

I had an urge to run.

'Look at this,' Kit was saying, 'I got far too much orange juice at the shop.'

*What are we going to do now? said the little boy. We're all alone.*

'The forecast says there's rain due.'

Just then, as if the sky had heard, the first few drops detached themselves from the expanse of white.

My book. I wanted to hug my book.

'Would you look at the time?' Kit said, though she hadn't taken her eyes from the sky and from what I could make out she wasn't wearing a watch.

I huddled in the doorway, imagining I could hear the Panda bumping its way down the track. Glasgow. I could have spent the day wandering the shops, watching people in the street and out the windows of cafés.

The rain was coming down in strings.

'Come on, then.' She tucked the carton of orange juice under one arm; it was the smooth variety. No bits. She beckoned me with the other arm.

'I haven't eaten anything today and my blood sugar's heading south,' she said. 'Let's go inside.'

# Meet for Fun

We were out together, Alex and me, when I got the call about my father. We sat down on a bench at a bus stop as I put my phone away. For a moment I considered not telling him. He might try kindness, which I didn't want – it was the last thing I needed – or he might make his excuses, get on the next bus.

We had only known each other a couple of months. We were having fun. That's what we'd put as our profile captions online: *meet for fun?* I thought I wanted nothing more than his fun.

'My dad's... not great.'

The news that he'd been hospitalised wasn't a shock. He had gradually lost interest in food and company. On the phone, my mother couldn't keep the alarm out of her voice. 'Your father always had an appetite like a child's,' she whispered. The last time I saw him he was so small and fragile I had to gather myself before I touched him.

Alex put a hand over mine, and for a good while we stayed like that, with me holding his hand in the middle of the street, not saying anything. We both noticed the length of the silence at the same exact moment, and then Alex gave my hand a squeeze and lifted away and I gathered myself, and later, I could still feel the soft pressure of his hand in mine.

When I got back to London after the funeral, I waited a couple of days before texting.

*I was literally just about to text you!* came the swift reply.

He came over that evening. He stood in the doorway of my flat with his head down, hands clasped below his chest, so he looked like he was praying.

'Made it, then.'

He stepped just inside the hallway and his after-shave was suddenly everywhere. I went to give him a peck. He curled his arm around me.

'Your dad... I'm sorry.'

'It's fine, look.'

'You're chittering.'

'It's cold, right?'

I didn't want him to let go.

'Let's get stinko,' Alex said, pouring the red. He asked how my mother was doing.

'After the funeral, she just... wouldn't stop talking,' I told him.

The sound of her voice was an emollient that she applied endlessly to her wound.

'Do you remember how he taught you to swim?' she'd said. 'It was something he'd looked forward to – he sometimes spoke about his own dad taking him to Lochindorb, the way the old man pulled him out into the cold water by his fingertips.'

The skin under her eyes pleated.

'You were a natural, Jamie. You talked across your dad's instructions and tried to wriggle out of his grasp. *I can do it by myself! I can do it!* I can still see you now, your big head wobbling on that wee body. When you came out of the water you were shivering. Your dad got you all wrapped up in a towel, then he pulled you onto his lap. He held onto you while you warmed up. Mind?'

She moved on to the next thought, without a breath, but I remembered. I mean, I remembered the sensation of being held if not quite the date and time.

'If I close my eyes, I can remember it now,' I told Alex. 'His warmth reaching every part of my body.'

'What will your mum do now?'

I looked at him. 'She'll keep going.' I took a sip. 'She has friends – she'll keep going. She'll probably live to a hundred-and-twenty.'

Alex nodded.

'When my dad retired, the folk in his office bought him a chair,' he said. 'It was one of those ones that recline if you sit back and lift your legs. I've got this image of my dad sitting in that chair in the mornings, just looking out the window and holding his cup of coffee, not saying anything, just staring out. Still and all he looked... serene. I think I was the only one of us who noticed how quiet and introspective he'd become. He didn't complain, though I saw him take a breath whenever he got up out of that chair. He wasn't eating much, come to think of it. Started shrinking away. Skin and bone. Took him about six months to die.'

Alex took a long drink. 'I never did get to grips with his language,' he added. 'He tried teaching us wee bits of it. I was never much interested – it was too hard. Whenever he switched away from English it felt like he'd turned into someone else, a stranger.' He stared ahead. 'We never got to grips with one another, my dad and me.'

I wanted to reach over and push the hair out of his face.

'I remember once we were all playing out in the street, me and a bunch of the kids from round about. We'd been raiding someone's dressing-up box and I was decked out in this lovely red number – maroon it was – all the way down to the ground. And I had this wee bow in my hair, one of those dicky bows with the elastic band. Thought I was the bomb. I must have been about five or six, sashaying down the street with my head high. And one minute my dad's face was there at the window and the next he was out in the street making a beeline for me, just flying towards me, getting bigger and bigger. I came to a stop, I couldn't move, and everyone else seemed to just bugger off and next thing my dad's got his hand out, he's got a hold of that bow, his face all scrunched and mean, and he didn't speak, he just pulled that bow back as far as it would go, and then – bang – back it came.'

He pushed on quickly, as though I'd tried to interrupt.

'Thing is, he wasn't a bad man, he wasn't cruel. We just didn't get each other.'

He sighed.

'Sorry,' he said. 'Sorry.'


Beside me later that night, Alex lifted and dropped, quite peaceful now. I got out of bed and pulled on my dressing gown. In the living room I unearthed a CD: King Creosote, 'Your Young Voice'. The music lilted into the room. It twisted itself around my innards. I reached for the switch.

I stood for a while at the window, looking down on the street as it widened out on to Garthorne Road.

The scene trembled in the rain. I could just make out a karaoke 'American Pie', somewhere nearby, the voice way out of kilter with the backing track.

The floor creaked behind me.

'Uh... Hi.'

Alex padded into the room, his shirt halfway up his arms.

'Any idea the time?'

For the first time in god knew how long I had no idea of the exact time.

'Early start?'

'Those maisonettes won't clean themselves. Man, this flat.' He squinted into the empty corners. 'How long you been living here?'

'Work in progress. I'll get there.'

He dipped his head, finding his shirt buttons. He'd no reason to stay the night. That's what fun is all about. It's all about not waking up next to someone else's musty breath; not making chat over the coffee.

'I'll phone later,' he said. 'If that's okay.'

He moved through the door, towards the stairs, the dark swallowing him.

I pushed the button on the stereo and King Creosote came back on, whispering to the end of his song, and I drifted off and woke and dozed again and got woken by the silence at the end of the CD. I listened to the traffic burping up the hill. Closed my eyes and, somewhere before the next sleep got me, I heard something, a glimmer behind me, a word or two slipping over my shoulder. I sat bolt upright and glanced towards the door but there was nothing there. I checked again, just to be sure.

*Dad?*

# Callum and Daisy

Kit discarded her coat on a chair by the front door. Underneath she wore a formless cardigan over a yellow football top. A bobbled badge. *BRASIL*, it said.

'Oh, this is one of Terry's old things,' she said without turning.

I followed her down the hallway. The wall to my right told a story in gallery form, beginning in an era when people sat stiff and unsmiling, progressing all the way to pouting and peace signs.

There was Kit, an infant with a muted smile, her hands clasped in her lap. Further on I saw her with darker hair, and then it grew shorter, lightened again, eventually turning that violet shade hair passes through before it finally admits to grey.

'I was nice-looking, wasn't I?'

'You haven't changed.'

'Oh, I'm happier now.'

She had placed herself before another picture, a family grouping, not posed, but formal seeming in its solemnity.

'My mother,' Kit said.

She was seated in the middle: fine-boned with scrunched eyes and iron-grey hair pulled back in a ponytail, a high colour to her cheeks like her daughter, though her face looked neither young nor old. Her husband, on her left, sat with his chest puffed high. He confronted the camera with Kit's near-colourless eyes.

Kit, I could see, was standing behind them, her arms loose at her sides. Then there was another young woman sitting on the floor at her father's feet, her knees at her chest, her arms hugging her knees.

All four smiled with suspicion, and although they were ranged close together there was a sense of separateness, as though their individual portraits had been photo-shopped together.

'I've no idea who took that picture,' Kit said. 'We lived out in the country – and by that, I mean down a track in the middle of nowheresville. My father was a farm worker and we never really had visitors or visited. We believed in keeping ourselves to ourselves. We did go to church, though. *Religiously.*' Her heels lifted at the joke. 'Maybe it was someone from our church. Or the minister or his wife.'

She turned, nodding as though I'd asked a question.

'Oh, they were very religious people, my parents. They were *decent* and very hard-working and all of that, but they believed in the Word, and they could be very strict. We had to work hard around the house and say our prayers and address them as *sir* and *ma'am*. Can you imagine? Just look at my sister's face: she couldn't be demurer if she tried. She could dial it down when she needed to. I'm sixteen and she's fifteen there. She's ready to fly.'

Kit gazed at the picture. 'Well now, come on through.'

She continued slowly along the hallway while I surveyed a diamond-shaped display of school photos: brash individual portraits of a boy who grudged smiling the older he got, interspersed with class gatherings. My favourite was his first school portrait. I loved its clarity, the fierce blue backdrop, his scratchy cable-knit jumper, the toothy smile, and blade-straight side parting that made him look like a child of the fifties, though the date underneath said 1975.

This thread continued onto a low table at the end of the hallway, where the same boy, heavier everywhere, posed with a young woman and a circumspect toddler, one hand from either parent holding him in place.

I looked up in time to see the tail of Kit's cardigan flapping through an opening on her right. This was the kitchen, with a shy glow coming in through French windows at the far end. Everything here was of pale wood, solid and clean. Metal utensils hung in a row above the cooker, tallest to shortest, like the line-up of shame before the sides are picked in gym class. A shelving unit filled with cookbooks, pleasingly worn, and bookmarked with differently coloured flashes of paper. Stairs leading who knew where, the lower steps piled high at the edges with paperbacks. It was very her, a happy, cluttered place.

As I turned my eyes around the room a large, framed photo, hanging not quite straight on the wall, assaulted my attention. It was the boy again, very much a man, with his family, two children now, almost teenaged.

She marched around the breakfast bar and began pulling glasses from a cupboard above her. There was a mechanical rhythm to her movements. She lifted a bottle the size of a bell jar from the cupboard.

'Let me know if you feel the cold. It's no odds to me. I'm a warm-blooded creature so I tend not to put on my heating until my toes start turning blue.'

She smiled as she slopped the cloudy liquid into a pair of glasses. It was pungent, sickly-sweet, a throwback to another era. Suddenly, she looked up.

'Oh now, I should have offered you a grown-up drink. I'm so used to my morning routine. Ginger beer wakes me up like a cold shower. One thing about me is I have a real sweet tooth. It's a miracle I've never needed a crown.' She waved over at the stocked wine rack. 'Or you could have a proper drink. I know it's early, but what the hell. Maybe later, then.'

After rustling for a moment in the bread bin she lifted out a couple of croissants, which she tipped onto plates.

'The chair with the high back is mine, for my posture.'

I took my plate and held my nose to my glass. Kit angled round to look at me full on. 'So, Alex!'

'He's auditioning for a documentary series. Radio.' I picked the end off my croissant. 'I'm just... He could really do with a break.'

'He's so good-looking. Like a real actor on TV.'

'Can I ask? Is that your son?'

'That's Terry. And Paula. They're *married*. And Callum and Daisy. *Daisy*' – she made a face – 'like a duck or a cow...'

'He's like you. Terry.'

'It's the chin, right?'

She leaned to the side, contemplating the picture.

'I'm not his *mother* mother, of course.' Then, seeing my face, she added: 'I mean, in the most important sense, of course I am, really I am, but the fact is, I wasn't the one who, you know...'

'Ah...'

'It was my sister Annabel who...' She mimed something large and heavy exploding out of her stomach like the creature in *Alien*.

'Oh. Wow. I mean...'

'It's quite the story. I don't want to keep you...'

For a moment I tried to look noncommittal, then shook my head, adjusting myself in my chair, all the time in the world.

'So, Annie... My sister was really her own person. So was I, you know, I always had a very clear idea of who I was, but I had something that she didn't. *Patience.* I could wait. Neither of us wanted the life my parents had planned for us, which was basically the life they had: lots of hard work and thrift and everything in its proper place. And church. So much church.'

She lifted her eyes to the ceiling.

'Funny. I'm not religious at all. I think I stopped believing in God finally when I was about sixteen, but whenever I think or talk about my parents or any of the dead, I always raise my eyes...' She jabbed a finger heavenwards.

I shuffled in my seat, resisting the temptation to look up, half-expecting to see the couple from the photograph levitating above our heads.

'Let's just say that my sister Annabel was not prepared to wait for her life to begin. She could only bide her time until my parents were in bed – which was always early, we're talking nine thirty latest – and then she'd climb out of our bedroom window and walk down the road to a waiting car, and she and her friends would take off for some clearing in

Bain's Woods and later on for Toronto, where I'm told it was cafés and parties until all hours, and I'd wake to her coming back through the window like Peter Pan at dawn with eyeliner running down her face, reliable as the sun. I didn't mind. I liked that I was her accomplice. I would have done anything for her, my sister. Well, you saw the picture: she was a knockout, right?'

She made arms towards the kitchen counter.

'Would you like another drink? There's everything. You've hardly touched your ginger beer.'

'It's just...'

'Disgusting, right!'

She held out her hand for my glass. I reclined while she chewed her way to the end of another mouthful. The armchair was so vast that my feet barely reached the floor. Or maybe I had shrunk.

'My sister was a whole load of different people, of course she was. As was I, but I was willing to play the game, you know?'

She tapped at her plate, gathering flakes.

'Annie didn't know she was pregnant until it was too late. Our mother knew what was happening before she did. My sister's blouses and billowing dresses were all the rage, but that bump told its own story, and then, well, everything changed.' She shuddered, recalling. 'It was terrible, their anger, but it was... the whole thing was so very sad. The worst of it was the way our parents had suddenly to let in a different reality, one that in no way corresponded to how they had always believed things were meant to go. That's what really hurt my heart.'

She was speaking as much to herself as to me, but there was something fluent and compelling about the way she told her story. For all her protestations, I could imagine her before a congregation, sermonising.

'Their *genius* plan was for my sister and my mother to disappear west to Alberta for a few months so that my mother could pass off the baby as her own. All fine in theory but Annie just didn't have it in her to play along. The minute they'd calmed down enough to take their eyes off her, she heaved herself and the bump out of that window – it was quite a sight; we were in cahoots, of course – and within a week everyone – school, church, all my father's co-workers – was talking about Kenneth Ross's girl, who'd got herself knocked-up at sixteen... And so, we had to move.'

Kit hugged her cardigan around her.

'But there was Terry,' she said, smiling. 'It was my father's middle name, Terence, and when he was born Annie... she *tried*, you know, she really did try. I can remember her bathing him in those early days, and she seemed fascinated by the smell of his head and his tiny hands and feet, but she was so easily bored.'

She sat forward. 'I'm not boring you, am I?'

I shook my head.

'Well, Annie never did have all that much of an attention span. All her teachers said she was easily distracted, right from the get-go. She withdrew little by little, left the rest of us to feed Terry and hold him, and make a fuss, and then she withdrew some more. Who knows how much of a chance she gave herself; you know? To be his mother? They hadn't a hope. And then one day she went out the front door and down the road and got into one of her friend's cars – not so much of a car, I think it was a kind of van thing they all slept in – and off she went.'

Kit peered down at her palms, as if the rest of the tale might be contained somewhere along the lifeline.

'Annie was carrying a bag, a stuffed shopping bag. I thought she was just getting out of the house for an hour. Fresh air. Going browsing or something, only the bag was already full, and the nearest shop was two miles away. I should have known she wasn't coming back by the fact that she went out the front door. Whenever she went out by the window she always came back.'

She laughed, but it was a forced laugh, as though she couldn't quite believe the story she was telling.

'I didn't mean to become his mother. Terry. I had my own plans. It was finally my time. Off I went, as planned, to my nursing college in Toronto, but whenever I came home, I saw my father and mother with this boy, this beautiful boy, and the way they were with him... oh, they loved him, but they were *tired*. And they were angry. They were angry for the rest of their lives. And I would lie in bed at night thinking it all over and I saw Terry disappearing out some window after Annie in the not-too-distant future, desperate to know who he was, hurting them all over again.'

She shrugged, her head lowering. For a moment I wondered if she would speak again.

'Of course, my father wore himself out with his anger,' she said, 'it was quite the sight, but I had made up my mind, there was nothing they could do, I was bigger than them. They ranted and threatened but they didn't dare set foot out of their corner. They were tired, and, in their hearts, I think they were relieved.'

Again, she glanced up at me for my reaction. I just nodded.

'And, as I was heading for my car, with Terry there holding me by the hand, with his little backpack on, it hit me hard. *My god, this is going to be so hard.* But maybe this was what I was supposed to do. Terry mattered. Of course, it would be hard – and let me tell you, it was *hard* – but I had to try. I knew I had to try.'

She looked up again, looked at me with such concentration that I had to turn away.

'I mean, it's all hard, Jamie.'

She lowered her glass and got to her feet.

'Take a gander at this.'

It was a Dictaphone.

'I've been recording myself. I've been telling myself stories. I want to get it all down before my memory goes to mush. Maybe there's a book in there, who knows? It's not such a remarkable story.' She laughed. 'If I'm honest, I'm getting a little tired of the sound of my own voice.'

I took the little device from her and lifted it towards my mouth, breathing deep, as though about to launch into my own confessional. I could feel her watching me, and for some reason my heart slowly tightening.

I sat up.

*I'm fine.*

'I keep asking myself: *is this the truth or is it just the story I hold in my head?*' she said, holding out her hand for the Dictaphone. 'And what does it matter now, anyway?'

She went back to the drawer and started lifting out leaflets, booklets of coupons, scraps torn from magazines. She plunged her hand right to the back.

'Got you!'

She unfurled a tightly wound plastic pouch, rummaging again until she unearthed a packet of fag papers.

'Come on, then.' She ushered me towards the French doors, and when I hesitated she gave me a look as if to say: *silly boy.*

Outside the rain had stopped. The sky was clear, but the garden was in the shadow of the steading and so dark you could barely make out the length of the lawn or the shape of the forest beyond. My thigh met the back of a wooden bench as I stepped out onto the patio. Kit flicked a switch and the lawn materialised before us. We leaned to see. The portion closest to us had been dug into furrows.

'I decided last year that I was going to plant a vegetable patch.' She frowned at the disturbed earth. 'Work in progress.'

I huddled in my corner of the bench as Kit fashioned the joint, her hands as steady as slate. When she was finished, she took a strip of hotel matches from her cardigan pocket and struck repeatedly until one wobbled into life.

She kept her attention on me as I drew the smoke into my lungs. I handed back the joint, and again our eyes met. She was sitting directly beneath the garden light. The white of her hair seemed almost to glow.

I felt her shift across the bench towards me and it was only then that I realised I was crying.

'I'm fine... I'll be fine.'

I swiped a hand across my face.

More tears – a flood.

I wiped and wiped at my cheeks.

'Sorry, I'm sorry. Thought I was such a big man. I used to have all this stuff I *had* to do…'

My mouth was open; my vision was blurred. I put a hand to my face, but I couldn't stop the outpour.

'What if I forget the… shape…?' I managed to say. 'What if I forget the shape of them?' A great sob. 'I'm so sorry, you don't know me…'

Kit handed me a tissue and I cleaned my nose while she waited, and I couldn't help myself, I started talking, the whole long story punctured with apology, and then I pressed my lips, desperate not to cry.

She waited.

'There are days when it feels like they're everywhere around me,' I said. 'I sometimes feel they're watching over me. I mean, I'm not… I'm the same as you, I don't believe in anything, I'm a downright atheist, but…'

'Superstition…' She shrugged.

'Sometimes it feels like they're looking out for me, watching over me, and sometimes, it feels like they're looking down and seeing things about me that they won't, you know…'

'We all feel like that sometimes. Every one of us feels like that one time or another.'

'I should at least have had the chance to thank them.'

'No need.'

I was crying again. She took my hand, pulling it into her lap, pressed her other hand down on mine.

'And I know they would have wanted me to...'

'Keep going. Yes.'

'I don't want to forget,' I said, my voice quiet. 'I don't want them becoming just people, you know, people whose faces I can barely recall.'

'You won't forget,' she said, and as I closed my eyes I saw the two of them, my mother and father, photo-real, dream-real: those thrice-weekly phone calls, heads pressed to the receiver, their lack of complaint or intrusion.

We sat for a long time gazing out across the garden, until something had to be said.

Kit shuffled in her seat.

'I remember when my father died. Oh, this was years and years ago now. I came back here to Scotland after the funeral and that first night home, in my bleary state, I saw my father standing at the end of my bed, leaning over, as clear as you are to me now. And it was... so weird, horrible at first, but I couldn't look away. It really was him, my daddy, in one of his light denim shirts and a pair of blue jeans. The farmer's shoulders he'd lost at the end of his life had grown back.'

She sat back, remembering.

'And as I watched, my father opened his eyes wide and he touched the side of his head like was trying to retrieve a thought or a plan of action. Hair silver and buzzed, neatly tailored sideburns going grey. Just the way it was before I even knew about his illness. He seemed so large. Larger than life I suppose you'd say, a giant version. I felt calm suddenly. I wanted him to scoop me up in his arms.'

Once again, she mimed the action.

'Later on, I wondered if he'd shown himself to me as a minding. Look, Katherine, this is Kenny, your daddy. That guy in the hospital bed with the small head and the bug eyes and all the hair growing out of his ears? *He* was the imposter.'

She relit the joint, offered it. I shook my head.

'So, I was sitting by his bed the day before he died,' she said. 'I took one of his hands and it felt like taking the hand of a stranger. His fingers curled loosely around mine. I saw the shining eyelids, the mouth opening and closing, but I couldn't see my father. I looked and looked but I couldn't see him. So, he came back. He had stood at the end of my bed in his strong, firm body as a minding. *This is me.*'

She held up the spent joint.

'Who knows, maybe I'd had one too many of these?'

She pressed the butt into the arm of the bench, and I returned, with a jolt, to the present, to the half-tended garden and the woods beyond.

'I have so many questions I wish I'd asked them when they were here,' she said. 'Sometimes I wonder if I've ever remembered them right. There were times when it felt so strange to still be here and walking around when they were gone. It's hard, but you go on, don't you?'

She pulled herself up in her seat.

'You fold it all into you, all the things, good and bad, and you just go on.'

After a time, she rose and brushed flecks from her clothes.

'I have to get going. It's Wednesday, which means that Lindsay Bremner wants visiting, and she'll be needing pineapple cake to finish off her lunch, so I'll have to stop off en route.'

Part of me wanted to keep her there, talking, but I could tell from the way she was gathering the fag papers and matches that her mind had already gone forward to Lindsay Bremner and her need for pine-apple cake.

And it was fine. The day belonged to me. I had all that time, and for now that didn't feel such a scary thing.

Back we went, down the hallway, and this time I saw that one of the doors had a little candy-striped sign: *CALLUM AND DAISY'S ROOM*.

'They visited a couple of years ago,' Kit said. 'I did up this room for the kids. Bunk beds and cute wallpaper – it took me forever, and they stayed for a week. Afterwards I kept finding things: world's tiniest pair of dungarees, half-chewed rice biscuits. It's like they're still here somewhere, waiting to jump out.'

She ran a hand over the sign. 'It's my turn to visit but I keep making excuses.'

'Where are they?'

'Sacramento, California, but I don't like planes! See, Terry wanted to live near my sister. She's settled now and she's been married for twenty years – to the same guy! And Terry has all these half-brothers and sisters, and the kids have all these cousins...'

Kit laughed. 'My sister's a *square*. I wouldn't have believed it, but my sister is now all the things she never thought she would be. She's a matriarch.'

Her shoulders heaved at the thought.

'I'm happy for them.'

I searched her face, but there was nothing there, no trace of bitterness or resentment. She carried on gazing at the little coloured sign for a moment, her smile as full and fond as ever, before turning to show me out.

# The Only Thing to Do

In the apartment the first thing I saw was my phone. Friends. *Brian, Donald, Evie, Priya*: the names slid upwards like closing credits. I fired off a handful of text messages and then felt put out when there were no instant responses.

Today was Wednesday. Brian would be at his Pilates. Donald was a night owl so he would most likely still be in bed. Evie would be in the thick of year nine sculpture. Priya? Uncompromising Priya. She'd only repeat the same questions. *Have you been eating properly? Is The Boyfriend looking after you? What about your art, Jamie? What about art?*

I sat on the bed, watched from the windowsill by inanimate objects. I blew a raspberry at Baby Bear, who was eyeballing me. I wondered if it was too early to call Alex.

I don't know how long I sat there. I could have stayed put, I thought, until nightfall. Maybe this would be my life now. Money in the bank. All worries, all sadness gone. The freedom to do fuck-all.

I opened my book and pressed my face into the page. In that moment I felt close to them, though I knew they were nowhere nearby.

The scent of smoke would fade until there was nothing but a memory of it, and, who knew, maybe the book's meaning would fade. It would drop down through a box of stuff in my next home; it would get bashed and torn up by my grandchildren. It would get chucked or forgotten during some house-move or other.

No thought at first of what would come next, just the book in my arms, magnolia walls and the low buzz of the here and now. And then: a sensation, growing, of something grappling inside me, struggling to get out. I couldn't stop the sense that there was something else I needed urgently to do.

So finally, I ran back through to the bedroom and burrowed in my holdall, unearthing my sketchpad in an eruption of socks and underwear.

I had bought it new for the trip, with no real intention of using it. It took a while to push beyond the tetchiness I felt at how it hurt my hand to do this now, the disdain I felt towards my first drafts.

She started to come through in the eyes and the wing-mirror ears and the way that the pieces of her face seemed to coalesce around her smile.

I would post the picture through her door before we left.

*What are we going to do now? said the little boy. We're all alone.*

*We shall have to spend the night here in the forest, said the girl. It's the only thing to do.*

The sun had punched holes in the forest walls; the whole place had come up clear. I kept stopping to look. I spent the longest time staring at a discarded apple core that was almost dried to a husk. I stood for a while mesmerised by a gnarled tree, its branches flung wide. I crouched and stared down at its slit opening, trying to fathom its depths, wondering if there were rooms full of treasures deep in the earth. Warm. When I finally looked up the sun had sunk, and the forest was moving in again.

By the time I reached the village the gift shop was locked up and I realised I had no idea of the time. I kept walking, wondering what I would eat, until I saw a woman in regulation white struggling out of the chippy with black bags for the wheelie bin. I crossed the road and helped her offload.

'Watch your nice jacket, son,' she said, as I rolled the awkward bundles upwards.

I was hungry, still a little stoned. I ate handfuls of chips on my bench under the streetlight. I almost didn't notice my phone was buzzing.

*Alex.*

'How did it go?'

'Well, they want me back. Tomorrow. I can stay with Sarah and Jo. It's between me and one other guy. The producer said he's going to let it marinate overnight.'

'That's what he said?'

'I know, what a wanker. If I don't get this one, that's me. I'm done. I'm just done.'

I'd heard this line before. Maybe this time what he said was true or maybe there would be another audition, another call-back, another shot of hope, and his career would live to fight another day.

'Okay, break a leg.'

'You'll be all right?'

*We shall have to spend the night here in the forest. It's the only thing to do.*

'Hurry back,' I said.


As I walked back my head was all Alex, the way his shape changed when he took his clothes off, the surprise of all those strong-cut lines. Sometimes he would just stand or lie there in the altogether, wearing his imperfections, like *this is me, who really cares, get over it*, his mind on other things.

I often remind him of our second date, in the pub in Vauxhall, near where he worked. I was first to arrive. I kept checking my watch; scared I'd made a mistake. Alex was suddenly there, at the door, looking around. He looked younger than I remembered and absurdly cute in a checked shirt and bomber jacket. He shifted his weight between his feet and scanned the bar.

Maybe I was wrong about this, about him. But there was this moment, the childish feeling in my belly. Enjoy this, I told myself. Enjoy this feeling. Who knows, maybe this will turn out to be the best bit: the moment before it starts.

I lifted my hand and waved him over.

Alex remembers it differently.

# History

At the end of our week, we stopped in at Alex's mother's place. It would have been rude not to, he admitted, buoyed by the phone call he'd received that morning.

'No need,' he said, when I suggested stopping for supplies. There would be a fridge-load of food – he reminded me she lived on picnic items and coleslaw – and it was just about warm enough to sit out on her decking.

We celebrated Alex getting the voiceover. His mother brought out the Laphroaig to toast his success.

'Any excuse.'

They had the same hooting laugh. I took a picture in my head, so I could draw them later, sitting together and laughing.

Around the third drink Alex dropped in that he had been on the verge of quitting, that he had been *this close* to jacking it all in, and his mother leapt in with a list of helpful suggestions for things he could do instead.

As she spoke Alex smacked his mouth and rolled his eyes, grinning through thunder, and eventually he got up from the table, the scrape of his chair cutting her off mid-sentence, and walked back towards the house.

They had obviously played this scene before. Never had I seen that set of his face, like an over-tired child, primed to explode.

She fumbled for a cigarette.

'Sure, it had to be said.'

She shook her head and sniffed. We sat in awkward silence.

I should ask her about herself. Who was this woman, from Donegal, who had come to Glasgow as a student and ended up marrying an Indonesian man and having five children? This was the potted version of the story; the one Alex had told me. What was her version?

When Alex came back, he affected a light tread. Soon we got ready to leave. But he glanced towards me as we were headed out of the front door and seeing my face he turned and hugged his mother, pulled her close, kissed her on the cheek, and I envied him that contact, the deep pressure, all their shared history.

# Let Be

Sometimes I find myself missing things that never happened. More than once I have pictured Alex ducking through the door of their house, lighting up every room like Tinker Bell.

My mum wouldn't have known where to put herself. At first, the presence of this alien prince at her table would have unnerved her. She would have eaten more slowly than usual. She would have strained to take in his every word. He would have gone out of his way to put her at ease with his offers of help and interested questions.

My father would try his best, too. He would likely refer to Alex as my friend, as though we were two single guys sharing a bed for reasons of economy. To him we could only ever be Morecambe and Wise. Bert and Ernie. Tucked up in our jimmy-jams, sexless and unthreatening.

Maybe I would correct my father. *He's my boyfriend*, I would say, my voice murder. *My lover. My husband.*

Or maybe I'd rise above. Let be.

I love to look at Alex when he doesn't know I'm there. I love him in profile; unawares, walking head down, eyes half-shut, smiling to himself about something he's remembered. I love the bits of him he can't see: the lively crown of hair, the nape of his neck. A label is sticking out of his collar, or the tail of his shirt has come untucked, exposing underwear and skin, and the sight just about breaks my heart.

# Once Upon a Time

Whenever I think about Mum bringing my father home for the first time to meet my grandmother, I picture them either end of the sofa with the rounded arms and white velour cushions.

I paint in the details. The spotlessly clean room I imagine would have a few tasteful prints on the wall and a cabinet full of ornaments. My parents would have kept a respectable distance from each other, with my father occasionally daring to lay a hand in the gap.

My grandmother, this woman I never met, might have offered Dad a small glass of beer, which he would have accepted out of politeness, drinking slowly but steadily. There would be discreet but significant questions. 'Where's home?' (Answer: three streets away.) 'What does your father do?' (Answer: he works in a garage over on London Road, but we don't expect that to last.) 'What do you want to do with your life?' (Answer: a whole cascade of things – my father was never short of ideas.)

But this picture is all wrong. That scene never took place in that room or on that sofa. When my parents got together at a dance in the mid-sixties, my mother and her mother were still living in the flat in Restalrig with the ducks flying up the living room wall and what my mum always described as the perishing bathroom. It would be another ten years before they bought that sofa together. It stayed for years in the living room of our flat above my parents' shop.

My grandmother, tall and bracing, leaves the room to boil the kettle, signalling with a wave for my parents to stay put, and when they're sure they're alone they turn their bodies inwards, they reach for each other and they gaze down at their laced fingers, and this is maybe my favourite image of them, this picture of subdued hope.

# Acknowledgements

I owe the following writers an enormous debt for their advice and encouragement over the years: George Anderson, Sophie Cooke, Pippa Goldschmidt, Kevin MacNeil, Willy Maley, Theresa Muñoz, Mary Paulson-Ellis, Zoë Strachan and Daniel Sellers.

One of the greatest gifts you can receive as a writer is a sympathetic editor, and I'm lucky to have been guided and challenged through this process by the kind and talented Laura Shanahan.

It takes a large village to raise a small book, and I'm thankful for the love, enthusiasm and support of my friends and family, especially Ryan, Sean, Iain, Aileen, Isaac, and my parents, Mary and Bill, who gave me books and taught me to love stories.

Book club and writers' circle notes for the
Fairlight Moderns can be found at
**www.fairlightmoderns.com**

Share your thoughts about the
book with #TheOldHaunts

# Also in the Fairlight Moderns series